Happy New Year from Presents! One resolution the editors of Presents like to keep is making time just for themselves by curling up with their favorite books and escaping into a world of glamour, passion and seduction! So why not try this for yourselves, and pick up a Harlequin Presents today?

We've got a great selection for you this month, with THE ROYAL HOUSE OF NIROLI series leading the way. In *Bride by Royal Appointment* by Raye Morgan, Adam must put aside his royal revenge to marry Elena. Then, favorite author Lynne Graham will start your New Year with a bang, with *The Desert Sheikh's Captive Wife,* the first part in her trilogy THE RICH, THE RUTHLESS AND THE REALLY HANDSOME. Jacqueline Baird brings you a brooding Italian seducing his ex-wife in *The Italian Billionaire's Ruthless Revenge,* while in *Bought for Her Baby* by Melanie Milburne, there's a gorgeous Greek claiming a mistress! *The Frenchman's Marriage Demand* by Chantelle Shaw has a sexy millionaire furious that Freya's claiming he has a child, and in *The Virgin's Wedding Night* by Sara Craven, an innocent woman has no choice but to turn to a smoldering Greek for a marriage of convenience. Lee Wilkinson brings you a tycoon holding the key to Sophia's precious secret in *The Padova Pearls,* and, finally, in *The Italian's Chosen Wife* by fantastic new author Kate Hewitt, Italy's most notorious tycoon chooses a waitress to be his bride!

Bedded by...

Blackmail

Forced to bed...then to wed?

He's got her firmly in his sights and she's got only one chance of survival—surrender to his blackmail...and him...in his bed!

Bedded by...Blackmail

The *big* miniseries from Harlequin Presents®

Dare you read it?

Melanie Milburne

BOUGHT FOR HER BABY

Bedded by... *Blackmail*

Forced to bed...then to wed?

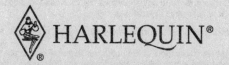

HARLEQUIN®

TORONTO • NEW YORK • LONDON
AMSTERDAM • PARIS • SYDNEY • HAMBURG
STOCKHOLM • ATHENS • TOKYO • MILAN • MADRID
PRAGUE • WARSAW • BUDAPEST • AUCKLAND

If you purchased this book without a cover you should be aware that this book is stolen property. It was reported as "unsold and destroyed" to the publisher, and neither the author nor the publisher has received any payment for this "stripped book."

ISBN-13: 978-0-373-12694-1
ISBN-10:   0-373-12694-8

BOUGHT FOR HER BABY

First North American Publication 2008.

Copyright © 2007 by Melanie Milburne.

All rights reserved. Except for use in any review, the reproduction or utilization of this work in whole or in part in any form by any electronic, mechanical or other means, now known or hereafter invented, including xerography, photocopying and recording, or in any information storage or retrieval system, is forbidden without the written permission of the publisher, Harlequin Enterprises Limited, 225 Duncan Mill Road, Don Mills, Ontario, Canada M3B 3K9.

This is a work of fiction. Names, characters, places and incidents are either the product of the author's imagination or are used fictitiously, and any resemblance to actual persons, living or dead, business establishments, events or locales is entirely coincidental.

This edition published by arrangement with Harlequin Books S.A.

® and TM are trademarks of the publisher. Trademarks indicated with ® are registered in the United States Patent and Trademark Office, the Canadian Trade Marks Office and in other countries.

www.eHarlequin.com

Printed in U.S.A.

All about the author...
Melanie Milburne

MELANIE MILBURNE read her first Harlequin
novel when she was seventeen and has never looked
back. She decided she would settle for nothing less
than a tall, dark and handsome hero as her future
husband. Well, she's not only still reading romance,
but writing it as well! And the tall, dark and handsome
hero? She fell in love with him on the second date
and was secretly engaged to him within six weeks!

Two sons later, they arrived in Hobart, Tasmania—the
jewel in the Australian crown. Once their boys were in
school, Melanie went back to university and received
her bachelor's and then her master's degree.

For her final assessment, she conducted a tutorial in
literary theory, concentrating on the romance genre.
As she was reading a paragraph from the novel of a
prominent Harlequin author, the door suddenly burst
open. The husband she thought was working was
actually standing there dressed in a tuxedo, his dark
brown eyes centered on her startled blue ones. He
strode across the room, hauled Melanie into his arms
and kissed her deeply and passionately before setting
her back down and leaving without a single word.
The lecturer gave Melanie a high distinction and her
fellow students gave her jealous glares! And so her
pilgrimage into romance writing was set!

Melanie also enjoys long-distance running, and is
a nationally ranked top-ten masters swimmer in
Australia. She learned to swim as an adult, so for
anyone who thinks they can't do something—you
can! Her motto is "Don't say I can't; say I CAN TRY."

To Margaret Seckold-Dodoo.
My best friend from senior high school,
who handed me my very first
Harlequin Mills & Boon® to read.

Margi, how can I ever thank you?
You started a lifelong love of romance and a
dream-come-true career. We don't see each other
often, but I will love you always!

CHAPTER ONE

As soon as Charlotte entered the boardroom she knew he had already arrived.

A shiver ran up her spine like a handful of mice making a tiny nest in the fine hairs on the back of her neck, as her eyes went to where he was standing.

As if he too sensed her presence, he turned his head and his coal-black gaze met hers for the first time in nearly four years.

Charlotte watched as he politely excused himself from one of the members of the museum board and came towards her, each one of his long strides making her throat tighten until she could barely breathe.

She had dreaded this moment for months, ever since she had heard that Damon Latousakis, the father of her little daughter Emily, was the principal sponsor for the Greek Exhibition she was helping the head curator organise for the museum.

Damon came and stood in front of her, his tall frame blocking her vision of the rest of the boardroom.

'Hello, Charlotte.'

She tried to disguise her nerves but her voice still came out creaky. 'H-hello, Damon.'

His dark gaze surveyed her in a leisurely manner, taking

in her chestnut hair, before dipping to brush her mouth, and then lower, lingering a moment too long on the hint of cleavage her velvet evening dress exposed, before finally coming back to her blue eyes.

Charlotte felt as if he had touched her all over, the electricity passing from his body to hers making her skin prickle and the air surrounding them begin to crackle with tension.

'You have done very well for yourself,' he said in a tone that suggested he hadn't expected her to. 'Under-curator, I hear. That is quite an achievement for a petty thief, but then—as you did to me—perhaps you have everyone fooled as to what you are really like.'

Resentment simmered in the tightening coils of her belly—the belly that had nurtured the child he had refused point-blank to acknowledge as his.

'I am the same person I always was, Damon,' she said with deliberate coolness.

His lip curled in disdain. 'No doubt you are, but I was too blinded by lust to see it at the time.'

Charlotte felt her face flame as a host of memories were unleashed by his use of that crude one-word description of what he had felt for her. The vision of the configuration of their bodies rocking in passion made her toes curl inside her high-heeled shoes. Her inner thighs quivered as she remembered how he had taken her to the heights of intimate pleasure time and time again on that two-month long study holiday on the Greek island of Santorini. The fiery heat of the summer sun and the blistering scorch of his passion had burned her to the core of her being.

Lust.

Damon had lusted after her while she had loved him—unreservedly and irreversibly.

'Excuse me, Mr Latousakis.' Diane Perry, one of the

museum staff, approached with a nervous smile. 'I hate to interrupt, but may I have a quick word with Charlotte?'

Damon gave her a smile that didn't quite reach his eyes. 'But of course,' he said and stepped back. 'I have finished with her.'

Charlotte watched as he turned and walked away, her stomach feeling as if someone had just kicked it with a lead boot.

'What was that all about?' Diane asked with a puzzled frown.

Charlotte forced her features into casual indifference. 'You know what Greek billionaires are like. They have arrogance down to a fine art.'

'Yes, well, arrogant or not, you'd better be careful with Damon Latousakis,' Diane warned her. 'I just got a phone call from Julian's wife, Gaye. Julian's been admitted to hospital with a suspected heart attack.'

'Oh, no!'

'He's going to be fine,' Diane assured her. 'But he is expecting you to keep Mr Latousakis sweet about this exhibition, especially as it now looks as if he will be out of action for a few weeks.'

'A few weeks?' Charlotte gulped.

Diane shook her head gravely. 'The doctors are suggesting he has angioplasty in a day or two. He will probably ring you himself and fill you in on what needs to be done, but in the meantime you'll have to take over the reins.'

'Me?' she squeaked.

'Of course you,' Diane said. 'You're the one with the most experience in Greek miniature sculptures. Besides, it was your idea in the first place to bring together contemporary artists and ancient works. This is the break you've been waiting for, Charlotte. It normally takes years working as an under-curator to get a chance like this. This will show everyone what a talent you have for set design and display.'

Charlotte felt her chest crumple with doubt. 'I don't think

I can do this on my own…Julian was the driving force behind all this. He was in contact with the sponsors. I had nothing to do with that side of things.'

'Rubbish. You'll be brilliant. You always underestimate yourself. You're one of the most talented people we have working in the museum.'

'Thanks for the vote of confidence, but aren't you forgetting something? I'm a single mum. I can't work the hours Julian was putting in.'

'Most of the work has already been done,' Diane said. 'But you'll have to make the welcome speech tonight. It's important you impress the sponsors, otherwise the exhibition might fall through. You know how competitive this industry is. Everyone wants a bite at the cherry.'

'I hate speaking in public…' Charlotte bit her lip. 'What if I stutter or have a mental blank or something? I always do when I'm nervous.'

'You'll be fine,' Diane said. 'Just have a glass of champagne before you start to calm your nerves. But remember to be especially nice to Damon Latousakis. He's the major sponsor as head of the Eleni Foundation. Without Mr Latousakis's funds and loan of artefacts from his family's private collection, this baby won't get off the ground.'

'It will be fine, Diane,' Charlotte said, her confident tone belying the fragile state of her emotions. 'I can handle men like Damon Latousakis.'

'Good,' Diane said. 'You've got about ten minutes to showtime. Why not go and sit in your office, away from the hubbub, to collect your thoughts?'

Charlotte opened her office door a short time later, her eyes widening in shock when she saw her younger sister in the process of making a bed with a threadbare coat on the floor.

'What on earth do you think you're doing?' she asked, closing the door with a little snap.

Stacey turned and gave her a vacuous smile. 'Hi, Charlie,' she said. 'I'm just having a little rest between jobs.'

Charlotte gritted her teeth, her brows snapping together crossly. 'I told you never to come here when you're in this state.'

'I'm not drunk.' Stacey pouted as she swayed on her feet. 'Just a little relaxed, that's all.'

'Where did you get it this time?'

'Get what?' Her sister's gaze tried to focus on Charlotte's but failed. 'You're such a strait-laced prig, you know that, Charlie? You ought to live a little. Get yourself a little buzz from time to time.'

Charlotte felt the cold hard fingers of despair claw at her stomach as she watched her sister's unsteady progress towards the nearest chair, her bottle-blonde head slipping sideways as she flopped down.

'Why are you here?' she asked.

Stacey looked at her through bloodshot eyes. 'I came to ask for a loan, but don't worry, I've sorted it out now for myself.'

Charlotte felt apprehension creep along her skin like the long thin legs of a stick insect. 'What do you mean?'

Stacey gave her a smug look. 'I ran into a rich Greek guy outside the toilets downstairs a few minutes ago,' she said. 'I offered him a quickie but he turned up his nose. He was such an arrogant bastard. I thought I'd teach him a lesson, so I pinched his wallet from his jacket as I brushed past.'

Charlotte swallowed the lump of dread that was suddenly threatening to choke her. 'H-have you still got it?'

'Got what?' Stacey's head rolled sideways again.

'His wallet,' Charlotte asked. 'Have you still got it or did you throw it away once you took out the money?'

Stacey squeezed her fingers into the back pocket of her

leopard-skin print jeans and tossed the wallet to her. 'I was going to give it to my mate Brian for his birthday. It looks like an expensive one.'

Charlotte's fingertips sank into the soft leather as she caught the wallet. She looked down at it for a moment before she opened it, her eyes going wide with horror when she saw the identification photograph it contained.

'Oh, no!' she gasped, her heart starting to clang against her ribcage.

Stacey lifted her head groggily. 'What's up? Do you know him or something?'

Charlotte closed her eyes for a second. Surely she had imagined it. She did this all the time, imagining she was seeing Damon Latousakis's face in every newspaper or magazine she opened. As soon as she saw jet-black hair, darker-than-night eyes and handsomely chiselled features her heart would leap to her throat. It was probably because she had just seen him, she reasoned—his features were fresh in her mind.

She opened her eyes and looked again, her stomach turning to liquid, her heart thumping so heavily she could barely inflate her lungs to breathe.

It *was* him.

She closed the wallet and put it in her evening bag with shaking fingers. 'How did you get into the building?' she asked.

'I told the guy at the front I was your sister,' Stacey said.

Charlotte suppressed an inward groan. Stacey's bottle-blonde hair was matted at the back and the jeans she had piped herself into were almost as indecent as the low-cut sweater she was wearing.

'Look, Stacey,' she said, glancing at the clock in panic. 'I have to give a speech in about three minutes.'

Stacey turned to her makeshift bed and began to bend

down. 'That's all right. I'm just going to have a quick nap before I move on.'

'No!' Charlotte pulled her to her feet. 'No, Stacey, you can't possibly sleep here. I might be ages and if anyone should find you in here…'

Stacey shrugged off Charlotte's hand and pouted. 'I get it,' she said with a downturn of her lip. 'You're ashamed of me. I'm not posh enough for your highbrow crowd.'

'That's not true… It's just that tonight's very important to me,' she said, trying to ignore the clock ticking on the wall, which seemed to be speeding up.

'Come on, Charlie,' Stacey cajoled. 'I only need a couple of hours sleep and I'll be on my way. I've got another client at eleven.'

Charlotte felt physically ill at the thought of her sister sleeping with whoever would pay her the money to do so.

'How can you do this to yourself?' she asked. 'Look at you, Stacey. You're stick-thin and so pale. You're slowly killing yourself and I swear to God I won't stand by and watch it keep happening.'

'I'll be fine in a couple of days… I just wanted one more taste before I give it up.'

One more taste.

How many times had Charlotte heard that empty promise? 'What about giving the detox clinic another go?' she asked.

Stacey pulled a rude face. 'That cruddy place. I wouldn't go there again if you paid me.'

'You get paid to go to lots of other cruddy places and to do God knows what cruddy things with no doubt totally cruddy men,' Charlotte pointed out irritably.

Her sister's lip curled. 'You're just jealous because you haven't had sex in close to four years.'

'Yes, well, look at the trouble it got me into when I did,'

Charlotte said and bit her lip as she thought of what Damon would do if he ever found out who had taken his wallet.

He was a flight of stairs away, waiting with all the other guests to hear her speak…

She released her bitten lip and said, 'There's a new private clinic in the Blue Mountains that's supposed to be getting good results. I read something about it the other day. It's frightfully expensive but would you agree to go there if I can rustle up the necessary funds?'

Her sister gave a non-committal shrug and slipped down even further on the floor. 'Maybe…maybe not.'

'Will you at least think about it, *please?*' Charlotte pleaded, tears of frustration beginning to sting her eyes. 'I don't want Emily to grow up without her aunt. You're all we've got, Stacey. Mum would be devastated to have seen you like this, especially after what happened to Dad.'

Her sister laid her head back on the cushion on the floor and closed her eyes. 'All right, I'll think about it,' she said grudgingly. 'But I'm not making any promises.'

No, none that you are likely to keep, Charlotte felt like saying, but instead quietly opened the bottom drawer of the filing cabinet and took out the bunny rug she kept for when Emily sometimes came in to work with her. She placed it over her sister's gaunt form, gently tucking in the edges to keep it in place.

Stacey made a soft sound and nestled down deeper, her sunken cheeks and lacklustre hair churning the dread in Charlotte's already tortured stomach.

Once she was certain Stacey was asleep, she retrieved the wallet from inside her bag. She looked at the photograph again, reeling under the flood of memories Damon's too-handsome features evoked.

Those black eyes had burned with desire from the first

moment they had locked with hers. She suppressed a little shiver when she thought of how that determined mouth had fed so greedily off hers. How his hands had known every curve and plane of her body and how his hard male presence had filled her with the explosion of his passion, taking away her innocence and leaving in its place an ongoing hunger that in spite of time and distance had never quite gone away.

She closed the wallet and suppressed a shuddering sigh. She would post it back to him anonymously at his hotel first thing in the morning.

Hopefully he would never find out exactly who had stolen it…

CHAPTER TWO

CHARLOTTE had only just closed her office door when a tall figure stepped out of the shadows of the corridor. She felt her heart leap upwards as the dark penetrating gaze of Damon Latousakis hit hers.

Oh, God, she thought in escalating despair. *Please, Stacey, don't make a sound.*

'I was wondering where you had got to,' he drawled as he came to stand right in front of her, his expression as inscrutable as a mask.

'Um...I had to see to some...er...paperwork,' she said, her throat feeling too tight to even swallow her rising panic.

'Is this your office?' he asked, indicating the door she was blocking with her body.

'Er...yes.'

'Why don't we go in and have a little chat?' he suggested. 'We have a few minutes before the board assembles.'

Her eyes popped in alarm and she pressed her back against the door. 'Chat about w-what?'

She stood stock-still as he picked up a long wayward strand of her chestnut hair and ran it through his fingertips as if examining the quality of a skein of silk.

'About us,' he said, his eyes burning with something she remembered all too well.

She felt the tremors of reawakened desire rearrange her insides, the hot lava of longing anointing her intimately and her breasts tightening as if they could already feel that hard male mouth sucking on them demandingly.

'Th-there's no us, Damon…' Her voice sounded like a rusty hinge opening. 'You ended our relationship four years ago, remember?'

'I remember everything,' he said, still playing with her hair, his coal-black eyes holding hers. 'And so do you. I see it in your eyes.'

The silence seemed to throb with memories, dangerously seductive memories that had the ability to destroy Charlotte's self-control all over again. She had thought herself immune to his devastating allure but, from the first time his dark eyes had sought hers that evening, she had felt the lethal tug of attraction in every one of her pulsing veins.

She suddenly heard the sound of a muffled cough from inside her office. 'I—I have to p-prepare for the meeting now…' she said hurriedly and with increased volume in case Stacey coughed again. 'I—I can meet you later, if you like,' she tacked on without thinking of the consequences. 'We can talk afterwards. You know…have a drink…or something…'

He released her hair and stepped back from her with an enigmatic smile. 'I will look forward to it, Charlotte,' he said.

She peeled herself from her office door once he began to walk back up the corridor, her chest almost collapsing with relief when he turned the corner for the stairs.

Agreeing to have a drink with Damon Latousakis had been her mistake four years ago; God knew what damage it would do to her now, she thought as she made her way to the boardroom on leaden legs.

Charlotte looked around the museum boardroom a few minutes later and wondered if she was going to need more than a glass of champagne for courage. The way she was feeling, a couple of bottles wasn't going to be enough to dull the panic racing through her system. Her stomach was threatening to misbehave and her head felt so tight she was sure her skull was going to crack under the pressure.

The late-arriving members and guests were finally milling in, their lively chatter setting her already frayed nerves on edge.

She could see Damon Latousakis standing at the back with a glass of barely touched champagne in his hand. He turned and locked gazes with her, the seductive promise she could see glittering there making her heart stumble in her chest.

'Members and honoured guests, ladies and gentlemen.' The museum manager took his place at the microphone, his booming voice thankfully kick-starting Charlotte's heart once more. 'It is our very great honour to have with us Mr Damon Latousakis, the head of the Eleni Foundation, who has travelled all the way from the beautiful Greek island of Santorini to be with us this evening.' He sent an ingratiating smile in Damon's direction before returning to the microphone.

'I would now like to call upon our acting museum curator, Ms Charlotte Woodruff, who is going to speak to you about how the exhibition cannot go ahead without the continued support of you—our members and our wonderful sponsors, including the very generous Mr Latousakis. Charlotte?'

Charlotte staggered towards the microphone, her mind going completely blank. What was she going to say? With the distraction of Stacey's impromptu visit and Damon's sudden appearance in the corridor she hadn't had time to prepare a speech.

Think! Think!

The microphone needed lowering to her height of five

foot five, which gave her a few precious seconds to get her brain into gear.

'Members and honoured guests, ladies and gentlemen…' she began and somehow continued her speech without once looking in Damon Latousakis's direction, but she could feel his black diamond gaze on her all the same.

Finally it was over.

She stepped down from the podium on legs that felt like not quite set jelly and took the glass of champagne Diane was holding out for her.

Diane spirited her away to a quiet corner. 'What did I tell you? You did a fabulous job. God, Damon Latousakis was looking at you the whole time like he was seeing right through that dress. You might think he's arrogant, but it sure looks as if you've taken his fancy.'

Charlotte took a deep slug of her drink, more to put moisture in her dry mouth than for Dutch courage. 'I'm sure you're mistaken. He doesn't like me one little bit,' she said, letting her worried gaze drift to where Damon was leaning down to hear what one of the board members was saying.

'What do you mean?' Diane frowned as she followed the line of Charlotte's vision.

'I've got a bad feeling about this,' Charlotte said, gripping her glass even more tightly.

Diane gave her a probing look. 'Have you met him before?'

Charlotte didn't answer but her expression must have given her away for Diane suddenly crowed, 'I've got it! You met him in Greece when you went to do some research for your studies, right?'

Charlotte put her half-drunk champagne down on a side table and turned around so she couldn't see the man who had torn her heart from her chest.

'We have a past, yes. But I'd rather not talk about it. Sorry, Diane. It's just too painful.'

'Don't worry, my lips are sealed,' Diane said. 'Uh-oh, he's coming back over. I'd better scoot.'

'No, don't leave me!' Charlotte made a quick grab for her colleague's arm but it was too late. Diane had already been nabbed by one of the members, who was leading her away to show her something of interest on the far side of the room.

'It is time for you to fulfil your promise, Charlotte,' Damon Latousakis said, towering over her, his expression set in intractable lines. 'Let us go and have that drink, hmm?'

'Um…I…I'm not sure that would be appropriate right at this moment… I have some more people to see and—'

He stepped closer so she had to crane her neck to keep eye contact, which she could only assume was a deliberate attempt to intimidate her. He had always used his exceptional height to his advantage and now was clearly no different. He towered head and shoulders over everyone else in the room, but with him standing so close she felt even shorter than she really was. And not just shorter, but stripped of any scrap of power she had fooled herself into believing she had.

'You are not reneging on our arrangement, are you?' he asked.

'I—I'm not sure it's such a good idea to revisit the past…' She moistened her mouth and added shakily, 'I've had a long day and I think it might be best if I go straight home…'

His eyes burned down into hers with a warning she knew was going to be impossible to ignore. 'Perhaps it would be a timely reminder at this point to inform you that if you do not follow through on your promise to have a drink with me, you could find yourself without an exhibition and, dare I say, without a job?'

It was true, Charlotte thought with a sickening wave of panic. If she did anything to compromise the exhibition's success her one-off chance at being head museum curator was going to remain exactly that—one-off. She would never be considered for promotion again and, as he'd intimated—perhaps even fired.

'The evening is drawing to a close,' Damon said. 'I have a limousine waiting outside. You and I will leave in it together and go back to my hotel, where we will have our private discussion and that little drink, understood?'

She swallowed the rough-edged lump in her throat. 'If you insist,' she said with undiluted resentment, her eyes flashing her ire.

'Good,' he said, taking her by the elbow. 'Let us go right away. Smile for the cameras, *agape mou*. It would not look good if you were seen in tomorrow's papers scowling at me as if I were the devil himself.'

Charlotte didn't trust herself to answer, but she could feel the touch of his fingers burn through the winter sleeves of her velvet evening gown, the subtle suggestion of force underpinning his hold striking a deep note of unease in her.

The stretch limousine was, as he'd said, waiting outside the museum's entrance and she made her way down the sandstone steps on legs that were struggling to keep her upright.

Once they were inside the car, Damon closed the panel separating the driver from the rear and joined her on the seat and his weight as he sat back on the plush leather caused her to tip sideways towards him. She put out a hand to stabilise herself but it landed on his strong, muscular thigh. She whipped her hand away but he caught it in mid-air and put it back down on his thigh, but much higher this time.

Charlotte's eyes flared with panic as she felt his body stir beneath her hand. She could feel her cheeks turning a hundred shades of red as she tried to ease herself away but he was having none of it.

'What is wrong, Charlotte?' he asked. 'Do you not

remember how you used to slip your hot little hand inside my trousers in the past? Is that what you were hoping to do tonight, touching me like that to remind me of what we had shared in case I had forgotten?'

She felt a burst of liquid fire explode between her thighs as a host of memories assailed her. Oh, God! He had taught her such intimacies. She had learned under a master, her body singing with the tune of his touch each and every time.

'And what about your equally scorching little tongue?' he continued, his eyes still lasering hers. 'Can you still taste me in your mouth, *agape mou*?'

She stared at him, unable to speak, unable to move, barely able to breathe.

He slowly brought his mouth to the side of her neck, his lips moving against her sensitive skin as he spoke. 'I can still taste you. Your saltiness and your sweetness are branded on my tongue.'

Charlotte's belly prickled with a thousand tiny needles of desire, her skin heating from the inside out. She tried to ease away but he continued his caress of her neck until he came to the upper curve of her right breast where the low-cut design of her gown gave him perfect access. She sucked in a sharp little breath as his tongue licked the exposed flesh, the faint but exquisite rasp on her skin sending every rational thought out of her head.

'You still taste of passion, Charlotte,' he said, his voice a low guttural growl as his hand reached for her bra-less breast. 'I can feel it beating beneath your skin.'

His hand took the weight of her breast while his thumb commandeered her already pert nipple, his touch hovering somewhere between pleasure and pain.

There was a hint of cruelty to his mouth as his head came towards hers, but she did nothing to try and escape it.

Just one kiss, she gave herself mental permission.

Just one kiss…

His lips were like fire on hers, his tongue an invading force as it ensnared hers in a duelling dance that sent her senses into overdrive. Her mouth clung to his, her free hand coming up to his head to bury her fingers in the black silk of his hair, her breasts pressed tight against his chest, her tongue flicking against his unashamedly and with escalating urgency.

He pressed her back into the leather seat, his mouth leaving hers to suckle on the breast he'd already freed with his hand.

Charlotte arched her back as his tongue curled around her nipple, the warm cave of his mouth pulling on her until everything went out of focus. She clamped her eyes shut and whimpered with pleasure as his mouth drew on her more fervently. She felt his erection swelling beneath her hand and, with a brazenness she had no idea she still possessed, she began stroking, up and down, until she had the satisfaction of hearing him groan his need out loud.

His mouth came back to hers, this time with a heat and fire that was devastating. It woke every sizzling memory in her brain of their passionate time together under the burning heat of the Santorini summer sun. Her head burst with the memory of swallowing him for the first time, relieving him of the unbearable pressure that even now she could feel building beneath the ministrations of her hand.

Damon tore his mouth off hers to stare down at her with glittering eyes. 'So it is as I suspected from the moment I saw you again. There is a fire still burning in your belly for me, as there is one in mine for you. It has never quite gone out, eh, Charlotte?'

She reared back in shock. 'No! That's not true.'

He caught her hand and brought it up to his mouth, his lips playing with each of her fingertips until he paused to ask, 'But the thing I would like to know is, what price have you put on yourself now?'

Charlotte looked at him, her heart kicking like an unbroken thoroughbred in her chest. 'P-price?'

His smile contained a hint of ruthlessness and his fingers tightened on hers. 'You have surely moved beyond the pick-pocket stage, have you not? You are after a much bigger haul this time around.'

'You're wrong,' she said, lifting her chin in pride as she tugged out of his grasp. 'I've never stolen anything from you or your mother. I was framed. I'm sure of it. Someone wanted me to be found guilty but it doesn't mean I was.'

'So you are still lying,' he said, his dark eyes flickering with anger. 'I would have thought you would have rid yourself of the habit by now.'

'I'm not lying!'

'I know what you are like, Charlotte. You are an expert at deceit. Four long years have passed and you are still the most convincing liar I have ever met. You do innocence so well I am sure you would confuse even a polygraph machine. But I am not a fool. I can see exactly what you are up to.'

Charlotte felt sick with apprehension. Her head swam with it, great swirls of it moving around so erratically she wondered if she might faint. She pinched the bridge of her nose to keep control, her whole body shaking beside the rigidity of his as the limousine drew to a halt outside one of Sydney's premier hotels.

'Get out,' he commanded as the doorman opened the door for her.

She got out on wobbly legs and came to where Damon was waiting for her, his hand reaching for hers, the latent strength of his fingers as they enclosed hers leaving her with no chance of escape even if she'd had the courage or lack of sense to try.

The lift began to sweep them up to the penthouse floor but

still Charlotte couldn't unlock her frozen throat. It was filled with the dry ice of dread as the number for each floor was illuminated by a bright green light. They should be flashing red, she thought as she swallowed convulsively again.

Red for danger…

CHAPTER THREE

ONCE the lift doors opened with a whisper, Damon pulled Charlotte along with him to his penthouse, swiping his card key and thrusting the door open so she could precede him into the plush suite.

She watched as he lifted his hand to his throat and released his tie, the action so very masculine she felt her stomach tilt sideways in spite of all that had happened this evening.

'What are you after this time around, I wonder?' he asked, shrugging himself out of his jacket and tossing it on to one of the luxurious sofas.

Her face flamed with a combination of fury and embarrassment. 'I don't want anything and certainly not from you.'

He gave a mocking laugh. 'Every woman is for sale,' he said with arrogant confidence. 'The trick for men is to get the currency right the first time around. You were after a billionaire husband four years ago and you very nearly pulled it off.'

His leather belt coiled like a serpent on the carpet and fear crept with frosty footsteps up the back of Charlotte's neck.

'But this time around I must say you have me a little intrigued as to your motives,' he went on musingly. 'You suggested we have a drink together but then you pretended you did not want to follow through. Then you could not stop yourself from touching and kissing me, and yet you deny any lingering attraction. You are playing cat and mouse games with me, are you not?'

'No, of course not!'

'You wanted to remind me of what I threw away, eh, Charlotte?' He lifted her chin so she had no choice but to meet his all-seeing gaze, his thumb stroking so close to her mouth she could feel her lips starting to tingle. 'Are you offering a re-run, I wonder?'

'No...' The word came out too softly to be believed but Charlotte knew that, no matter what passion still flared between them, she couldn't possibly sleep with him without revealing her emergency Caesarian scar. He had accused her of lying about her pregnancy to get out of trouble. What would he say when he found out she hadn't been lying at all?

If he were to find out she'd had his child, she knew she would be forced to say goodbye to her daughter for ever. She knew it without a doubt. With her sister's problems on top of what Damon had already accused her of four years ago, Charlotte's press for full custody would be laughed out of court for sure. Besides, good legal representation would cost her dearly and she had enough money worries already without adding to them.

She *had* to get Stacey into that clinic. It was her only chance to get out of the clutch of her addiction.

'You are looking pale,' Damon observed, dropping his hand. 'Have I shocked you, Charlotte? Did you not think I would still want you after all this time?'

She moistened her mouth. 'Y-yes...I am a little shocked...'

His eyes glinted. 'To tell you the truth, *agape mou*, so am I. I did not expect to feel anything but hatred when I saw you tonight but the sudden rush of desire I felt and still feel for you is like a fever raging in my blood. I will have you again.

That is what your little heat and retreat routine tonight was all about, was it not? To make me revisit what we started four years ago.'

She sent him a look of defiance overlaid with scorn. 'Only a barbarian would want to satisfy a desire for someone he hated.'

'You think me a barbarian?' His black eyes challenged hers. 'I can see I am going to have to make you eat those words, Charlotte. You were the one who came on to me in the limousine, remember? You made it very clear you were interested in resuming our association.'

Anger rose in her like bile; she could taste it in her mouth, the metallic sourness making her feel positively ill. Shame was there too, burning red-hot shame that leaked into her cheeks as she remembered how she had touched him.

'If you think you can intimidate me, think again,' she lied.

'I must not be getting my message across very clearly,' he said silkily, his deep voice moving over her skin like a flow of sun-warmed chiffon.

She disguised a nervous swallow but she saw the way his gaze dipped to her neck as if he had sensed the up and down movement of her throat. 'Wh-what do you mean?' she said.

'I want you, Charlotte as much as you want me,' he said. 'I am here in Sydney for the next month. During that time I want you to be my mistress.'

She reeled backwards in shock. *'No!'*

His dark brows rose imperiously. 'No?'

'N.O. No,' she repeated. 'Never.'

He paused for a moment, each second ticking by feeling like a hammer-blow to Charlotte's skull. The tension was unbearable.

'I met someone this evening,' he dropped into the taut silence. 'Someone who reminded me very much of you.'

Charlotte's eyes flicked nervously to her evening bag before she could stop them.

'It seems theft runs in your family,' he continued.

'I don't know what you're talking about.'

'The police are searching for your sister as we speak,' he informed her. 'Once they locate her, it is up to me to decide whether or not to press charges.'

She stared at him speechlessly, her stomach folding over in panic.

'Of course, if I do happen to press charges, she is likely to face trial, even be sent to prison,' he continued in the same coolly detached tone.

Charlotte knew all about prisons and the drug use that was rife within them. Her father had died a horrible death—a death that could have been prevented if he had received the help he'd needed earlier.

She *had* to stop the same thing happening to Stacey. Whatever it took, she had to stop her sister going down even further. Stacey would never recover, not after months in some horrid prison with heroin on tap.

'So you see it is all up to you, *agape mou*,' he said with another little unreadable smile. 'You either agree to be my mistress for the next four weeks or you will be seeing your sister from between iron bars for who knows how long.'

'You can't ask this of me. It's totally immoral.'

'Perhaps your sister's welfare is not enough inducement for you,' he said, his gaze sweeping over her indolently. 'I can see you have much more class than she has, so perhaps I will have to use a different currency with you after all.'

This is it, Charlotte thought with another sickening wave of panic. *Here goes my career and my livelihood.*

'Are you not going to ask me what I mean, Charlotte?' he demanded when she didn't respond.

She clenched her teeth until she was sure they would crack. 'All right, let's get it over with. Tell me what you're going to do if I don't cooperate. I can handle it. It is after all what I expect from someone as unprincipled as you.'

'You will have to tame that tongue of yours,' he cautioned. 'I will not tolerate you speaking to me in such a way.'

She tightened her mouth and glared at him. 'How do you expect me to speak to you when you're treating me like a…a…?'

'Whore?' he offered. 'Isn't that the word you are looking for?'

'I am not a whore and you cannot make me one.'

'I have no intention of doing so. The role I have assigned for you is somewhat different,' he said smoothly. 'You will be my companion for the many social engagements I have planned for the time I am here. I do not know my way around Sydney and would appreciate your company.'

'And if I don't agree to this preposterous plan of yours?'

He smiled another one of his enigmatic smiles. 'I would have thought you would have worked that out for yourself by now, *agape mou*.'

She *had* worked it out but she clamped her lips tightly together and waited for him to continue, her stomach tightening with apprehension.

'If you do not consent to be my mistress, the Eleni Foundation will immediately withdraw its sponsorship from the Greek Exhibition you and your desperately ill colleague have meticulously planned. Of course, if the major sponsor should pull out, what do you think the other smaller ones will do?' he said.

Again Charlotte knew exactly what they would do, but wasn't going to give him the satisfaction of hearing her say it out loud.

'As to your job…' He paused to inspect his signet ring for a moment before returning his gleaming eyes to hers. 'Is it worth losing over a simple matter of your pride?'

She tightened her hands into fists. 'You can't do this. I won't let you toy with me like this.'

'The way I see it, Charlotte, you do not have any choice. You either agree to be my mistress or face the consequences. I let you off lightly four years ago. My mother was far too gracious on your behalf to allow me to send you to the authorities as I had planned.'

Her eyes shone with unshed tears.

She *would not* cry.

Not now.

Not in front of him.

'I did not steal from your mother's gallery.'

He ignored her to continue, 'You wormed your way into my bed in order to get to the treasure trove of my dead father's priceless collection, did you not? I should have guessed it but I was naïve to the underhand tactics of someone like you. You had me fooled, which is something I am not proud of to this day. I foolishly fell for a lie. I had you picked as a young, innocent twenty-two-year-old student who had not seen much of the world, but I was wrong. You are as street-smart as they come, perhaps even more so. The hostel operator told me later that you had had at least two other men in your room while you were seeing me.'

She looked at him in outrage. 'That's an outright lie!'

He tilted his head at her imperiously. 'You have some other explanation?'

'Yes. The two young men in question were nothing but troublemakers. I met them a few days before I left. They were annoyed I wouldn't go out with them to party all night. They started playing practical jokes on me like leaving their clothes in my room or pinching my pillow.'

'You did not mention them to me at the time,' he pointed out with narrowed eyes.

'I didn't see the point. They were just kids with too much money and too little sense. I didn't want them to get into trouble unnecessarily.'

'I do not believe you.'

Her eyes blazed at him in fury. 'It wouldn't matter what I said—you'd never believe me. You're crazy. Totally out of your mind crazy.'

'Not crazy, Charlotte—I am simply in search of justice.'

'Why now?'

'When I was approached by Julian Deverell about this exhibition I was immediately interested,' he said. 'I knew you lived in Sydney, but when I found out that you not only worked at the museum but would be actively involved in the exhibition itself, I could not resist coming to see what you had made of yourself.'

She gaped at him. *You planned this?*

He gave her an indifferent look. 'It was too good a coincidence to pass up on. I must say it impressed me that you had gone on to complete your studies, even to get a Ph.D.—a grand achievement for a young woman of your age, but again, I imagine you slept your way to your graduation.'

Charlotte glared at him, her chest rising and falling in anger at his assumptions about her character.

She had worked so hard to get her final qualification. Her pregnancy had been a nightmare and her mother's sudden diagnosis of an aggressive type of breast cancer had made a difficult situation unbearable. She had studied into the early hours, existing on a minimum of sleep in order to get her thesis written, all the while nursing her rapidly failing mother and doing her best to keep her younger sister out of the trouble she seemed intent on drifting into with an unfortunate choice of friends.

Charlotte still blamed herself for Stacey's current problems. She had been too preoccupied with juggling her pregnancy and completing her degree to do what should have been done. Stacey had been steadily heading down the same destructive pathway as their father but she hadn't wanted to acknowledge it. It had been too painful.

'You can think what you like, but I can assure you my qualifications are all above board,' she bit out.

'Nevertheless you have used them to your advantage, have you not?' he observed. 'You handle daily some of the most priceless artefacts in the world. Tell me, Charlotte, have you been tempted to steal something from the museum and sell it on the black market yet?'

She threw him a caustic glare. 'I am not even going to dignify that question with an answer.'

'Why did you not tell me your father served a considerable time in prison for armed robbery?' he asked after a small but carefully timed pause.

Charlotte could feel shame weighing her shoulders down but forced herself to hold his obsidian gaze. 'My father died behind bars several years ago. I don't even think of him now.'

If he was in any way taken aback by the cold, unemotional delivery of her statement he showed no sign of it.

His eyes bored into hers for another beat or two before he continued in a tone that contained an unmistakable threat. 'It would be rather unfortunate if I were to be forced to reveal to your employers your little indiscretion of four years ago. They might not like the thought of harbouring a thief in their midst.'

Charlotte knew he would do it. She could see the ruthlessness in his dark-as-night gaze as it challenged hers.

'You are all I most despise in a man,' she said through tight lips. 'I cannot think of a man I hate more.'

'Then it will make our relationship all the more exciting, don't you think?'

'It will make it disgusting and unbearable,' she shot back.

'I will make sure you are adequately compensated,' he said

and reached for his cheque book in the inner pocket of his coat. 'You will need an array of glamorous clothes, for which I do not expect you to pay for yourself.'

She watched in sinking despair as he slashed his distinctive signature at the bottom and handed it to her.

'It's blank,' she said, glancing down at it without taking it from him.

'That is because you can name your price, *agape mou*,' he said. 'I am willing to pay you whatever you want. You, of all people, know I can afford it.'

Charlotte felt like asking for a totally outrageous sum but her pride wouldn't allow it. He had wrapped his proposition in the euphemistic term of mistress but she knew exactly what he was expecting in return.

A vision slipped into her mind of her sister taking money off strangers to feed her habit. Night after night Stacey rented her body and yet here was a chance for Charlotte to put an end to that for ever.

She skittered away from the thought of being Damon's lover again but the images came creeping back into her brain: his long, hair-roughened legs entwined with her smooth ones, his body pumping its frantic passionate response into the tender sheath of hers.

Her stomach gave a funny little somersault at the thought of feeling that level of sensuality again.

No.

She would not, could not, do that again.

'Since you are having such difficulty deciding on the amount, I will leave you to fill it in yourself,' he said and, before she could stop him, he took her bag from her shaking fingers and opened the clasp.

Charlotte's breath screeched to a halt in her chest, her face feeling as if a bonfire had been lit in each cheek as he took out his wallet, his long tanned fingers seeming to her as if they were moving in slow motion.

'I—I was going to give it back to you…' she said as his dark accusing eyes locked on to hers.

The white tips of anger about his mouth distorted his arrestingly handsome features into harsh lines of revenge. 'You lying, thieving little bitch,' he ground out. 'You are working as a team with your sister. I should have guessed.'

'No! That's not true!' she said. 'I'll g-get your money back for you…'

His brows snapped together in time with the closing of his wallet. 'Indeed you will,' he said. 'But in the meantime you can pay me back in kind.'

Charlotte swallowed convulsively. 'I can't do this, Damon,' she said brokenly. 'Please don't ask me to.'

'I'm not *asking* you, Charlotte—I'm telling you. If you do not agree to be my mistress, then your sister will face the authorities as she so clearly deserves.'

She felt her shoulders drop in defeat. It seemed there was going to be no way out of this.

'How much do you want?' he asked again, each hard-bitten word driving a stake through her heart.

She stared at the floor and mumbled what she thought would be enough to cover the cost of Stacey's rehabilitation—her face fiery red with shame at what she was committing herself to in agreeing to be his short-term mistress. It was a pathway to heartbreak all over again, but what other choice did she have? She could hardly tell him the truth about her motives. Stacey's issues aside, if he found out he had a child he would stop at nothing to take Emily away from her.

He wrote the figure on the cheque and handed it back to her. 'I can see how you have perfected the art of camouflaging your real motives. You give every appearance of being uncomfortable accepting money from me, but I know that is all a clever little ruse of yours to get me to lower my guard.'

'I feel uncomfortable accepting a glance from you, let alone anything else,' she said in arctic tones. 'The thought of sharing my body with you sickens me to my stomach.'

His black gaze visibly hardened, his jaw tensing as he fought for control. 'It did not seem to sicken you a short time ago in the limousine. We both know I could have taken you then and there.'

She knew it was foolish but she couldn't resist retorting, 'It would have been by force.'

He gave a mocking laugh. 'You think so?'

She sent him a fulminating look. 'I hate you, Damon Latousakis. I hate you with every breath and bone in my body.'

'I am sure you do, but perhaps I should make it clear at this point that your hatred and loathing is to be kept strictly private. In public we will be like any other couple who have nothing but the highest regard for each other.'

'And if I don't comply?'

'I am surprised you have the gall to even ask me that,' he said.

She lowered her gaze in case he saw the desperation she was feeling. 'How do you wish to…er…conduct our…relationship?'

'I would like to see you on a regular basis.'

Charlotte felt her insides twist in anguish. Her little daughter Emily hated it when she went out more than once or twice a week. It was hard enough juggling a day job without trying to burn the candle at both ends. And this particular candle was going to be a very dangerous one…

Damon looked down at her wide frightened blue eyes and frowned as his conscience gave him a sharp little nudge. Had he pushed her too far? He hadn't thought so but how could he tell? She was a master at deception and he wasn't going to allow himself to forget it for a minute. She had fooled him before with her declarations of undying love but she had betrayed him in the end. She had ruthlessly used her relationship with him to get to his family's wealth and that he would never forgive. Tonight was yet another example of her artifice. It could hardly have been a coincidence that her sister stole his wallet. Charlotte had known for months that he would be there that evening. What better payback for the way he had uncovered her thieving in the past than to do the very same again, albeit vicariously?

'I will expect you to be available to me each evening,' he said into the stiff silence. 'There will be late nights on occasion.'

She looked up at him, tears sparkling like tiny diamonds in her Aegean-blue eyes. 'I can't stay overnight…'

His hand tipped up her chin. 'Is there someone else?'

What could she say? *Yes, your little daughter, who will expect me to tuck her in each night.* It would be asking for instant heartbreak. She'd have to find some way of fulfilling his expectations of her without compromising Emily's well-being. It wasn't as if she could rely on her sister, but her friend Caroline Taylor was another option she could explore. They often traded babysitting time when either of them had something important on in the evening.

'No…no, there's no one else…' She had to think on her feet and added, 'I'm doing an on-line course on archaeology. I have to study most nights. I have assignments to complete… It's a big workload…' She held her breath to see if he believed her, his eyes raking her face as if searching for the colour of her lie.

He released her chin after an eternity and stepped back from her and held open the door. 'I will see you tomorrow evening,' he said, his voice detached and cold. 'Seven-thirty in the bar downstairs. I will make sure the concierge issues you with a swipe card to my room if I am not there to meet you on time.'

Charlotte walked past him on shaky legs. She turned around but he had already closed the door, the sudden movement of air feeling like a slap on her tear-streaked face.

CHAPTER FOUR

IT WAS only as Charlotte handed Damon's cheque over at the bank in her lunch hour the next day that she realised something was amiss. Her brow creased in a worried frown as she watched the teller process the transaction, the young woman's fingers flying over the keys as the funds were deposited into Charlotte's credit card account.

Why did Damon have an Australian bank account if he was only here for a month? But then she wondered if he'd made some arrangement with the bank after his wallet was stolen, for although his wallet had now been returned, she assumed he would have cancelled his cards when first realising what had happened.

She pushed aside the disturbing thought that he might be here for longer than a month.

That was just too terrifying to contemplate…

She left the bank and called her friend Caroline on her mobile as she walked through the park back to the museum.

'Emily was an angel as usual,' Caroline said once they had greeted each other. 'How was your cocktail party?'

'It was…stressful.'

'Well, you *were* thrown right in the deep end,' Caroline consoled her. 'I would hate to have to step into someone else's shoes like that at the last minute.'

Charlotte chewed her bottom lip for a moment before asking, 'Caroline, I have some…er…work stuff to see to this evening. I know it's a terrible imposition, but do you think you could mind Emily for another night? Something's…cropped up.'

'Of course,' Caroline said. 'Hey, you sound upset. Is everything OK?'

Charlotte hated lying to her friend but there was no way she could tell Caroline about Emily's father being in Sydney, or at least not yet.

'I am a bit,' she said. 'You know how I told you my boss Julian Deverell is having a heart procedure done?'

'Yes, that was a shock, wasn't it? Is he going to be all right?'

'As far as I know, but as a result of him being out of action I've been handed a whole lot more responsibility for the next month. I have to put in some extra hours and…and attend one or two functions in the evenings.'

'You know I am always happy to help, Charlotte. Us single mums have to stick together,' Caroline said. 'Janie loves having Emily here and, to tell you the truth, two is better than one. You know how only children can be so demanding at times. The girls play so well together it gives me time to catch up on my dressmaking.'

'So you really don't mind?'

'Of course not! But if you don't want to disrupt Emily's home routine night after night I could always get my mother to come over to your flat to babysit,' Caroline offered. 'You know how much she adores Emily and she certainly won't expect payment, so you needn't worry on that score.'

Charlotte wished she could have taken up the generous offer, but with Stacey coming and going from her flat in various states of disarray, she couldn't bear the explanations that would be necessary, especially to a woman of Caroline's mother's generation.

'I wouldn't want to bother your mum,' she said. 'Besides, it's only for a few nights and, as you say, Emily loves being with Janie. I'll pop over before I leave for my...er... function tonight to tuck Emily in, OK?'

'Don't worry about a thing,' Caroline said. 'You just concentrate on the job at hand. I'm sure you're going to totally wow them at your thingy tonight.'

Yeah, right. Charlotte grimaced as she stuffed her mobile back into her shoulder bag. The last thing she wanted was to wow anybody and certainly not Damon Latousakis.

'I can't believe you're doing to this to me,' Charlotte was close to screaming at her sister as she was rushing to get ready for her meeting with Damon.

She was going to be late as it was, having spent time with Emily before she'd raced back to her flat to tidy herself up a bit. Her little daughter had been over-tired and a bit tearful and Charlotte had felt so torn, having to leave her when it was clear Emily wanted to be with her. Stacey turning up on the doorstep with a yet another plea for money had been the last straw.

'I just want fifty bucks.' Stacey pouted at her.

Charlotte turned from the mirror where she was trying to insert an earring. 'Yes, but for what?'

Stacey gave a shrug. 'Food and stuff.'

'There's food in the kitchen, help yourself.'

'Come on, Charlie. I'll pay you back.'

Charlotte glared at her in fury. 'If you so much as dare to hand me money you've earned by sleeping with...' She stopped, suddenly realising how hypocritical she was sounding.

'What's with you this evening?' Stacey asked with a surly look. 'You're like a long-tailed cat in a room full of rocking chairs.'

Charlotte straightened her spine. 'I'm going out.'

Stacey's eyes popped. *'With a man?'*

Charlotte pursed her lips. 'Yes, just the one actually, nothing quite like your turnover, I'm afraid.'

Stacey whistled through her teeth. 'So who is he?'

'I don't have time to go into details—I'm running late as it is.'

'You should be careful who you go out with, Charlie,' Stacey said. 'There are some real creeps out there. I wouldn't want you to get into any trouble.'

Charlotte rolled her eyes. 'I know what I'm doing.' She stuffed her feet into her heels and smoothed down her simple black dress, her stomach growling with nerves.

Stacey got up to follow her out of the bedroom. 'And don't accept any drinks from anyone unless they have been opened by you or you've seen them poured in front of you. You could get spiked with a drug.'

Charlotte swung around to look at her sister. 'Why? In case I get addicted just like you?'

There was a tense little silence.

Stacey turned away, the stark outline of her thin shoulder blades beneath her close-fitting top making Charlotte's insides twist with guilt.

'I'm sorry…' she began.

Stacey turned and gave her a grim look. 'No, you're right. You're absolutely right. I'm an addict and I wish to God I wasn't. I just can't seem to get on top of it. I try and try but it's so hard…'

'Will you go to the clinic I suggested?' Charlotte urged. 'I've downloaded the details from the web and I've got the money to pay for it on my credit card.'

Stacey rolled her lips together without answering.

Charlotte decided it was time for a bit more pressure to be applied. 'I had a conversation with the man whose wallet you stole,' she said.

'That arrogant pig.' Stacey screwed up her face in disgust. 'How'd he find you?'

'That's immaterial,' she said. 'But he said he was going to press charges.'

Stacey's chin went up to a pugnacious height. 'Let him. See if I care.'

'Stacey, six weeks in prison, let alone six months or, God forbid, six years would kill you. You know it would. Look what it did to Dad. I want you to get out of town as soon as possible. You were lucky the police didn't find you last night. The clinic is totally confidential and totally remote and secure. No one will find you there. I'll make sure of it.'

Stacey let out a little sigh, her thin shoulders slumping in tired resignation. 'I guess I have no choice.'

'You don't unless you're ready to face the consequences of what you did. This way you can get away while the dust settles and detox at the same time. In a month you'll be a new woman, I guarantee it.'

'All right…'

Charlotte's heart leapt in relief. 'Really?'

Stacey looked down at her bruised pin-pricked arms and gave a rueful grimace. 'Yeah…I'm ready to get sorted out. Besides, I'm running out of veins.'

Charlotte gave her a bone-crushing hug and released her to press a soft kiss to her forehead. 'I'm proud of you, Stacey. I know you can beat this. And you don't have to face it alone. I'll be with you every step of the way.'

Stacey gave her another twisted little smile. 'I don't know why you've stuck by me this long. Most sisters would've given up long ago.'

Charlotte held her sister's cold, claw-like hands in hers and gave them a gentle squeeze. 'I would do *anything* to get you well again, Stacey. Do you understand? Absolutely anything.'

Stacey nodded, tears shining in her light blue eyes. 'Thanks…' She gave a big sniff and added gruffly, 'Now look what you made me do. You made me cry.'

Charlotte gave her another quick hug. 'I'll see you later. Have something to eat and watch some TV or something. You can share my bed or sleep in Emily's as she's staying with Caroline and Janie tonight. That way we can get you to the clinic first thing in the morning.'

'Thanks. I hope your date goes well,' Stacey called out as Charlotte bolted for the door. She gave a teasing smile and added, 'But don't let him kiss you, got that? I don't want you turning into a slut or something.'

Charlotte stretched her mouth into a smile that felt like an amusement implant. 'Got that,' she said and closed the door.

The hotel bar was crowded but Charlotte could feel the magnetic tug of Damon's gaze as soon as she entered. He was standing head and shoulders above everyone else, a drink of some sort in his hand and his usual inscrutable look on his face.

Nerves fluttered like a handful of moths in her stomach as she walked to where he was standing, her tongue sneaking out to run over her lips as she met the twin black pools of his gaze.

'Would you like a drink?' he asked without so much as a greeting, his eyes running over her possessively.

She raised her chin in pride. 'I would like you to greet me as if I was a normal date. I do have a name, you know.'

His dark eyes held hers for a moment. Then, placing his glass to one side with an exactitude she found a little unnerving, he took her by the upper arms and, tugging her towards his hard body, planted a hot, moist brandy-flavoured kiss to her mouth.

'*Kalispera*, Charlotte,' he drawled.

She stumbled backwards when he released her, her face aflame. 'I didn't mean like that!'

He raised his brows. 'Would you have preferred me to caress you as well?'

She let out a hissing breath and ground out in an undertone, in case the nearby drinkers could hear, 'I would prefer not to be here at all. Having you paw me in public would be the ultimate in degradation.'

A warning flickered in his black eyes as they locked with hers. 'Careful, Charlotte,' he said. 'I wouldn't want to have to spoil this evening by calling the police. Where is your sister, by the way?'

'I don't know where she is,' she lied. 'I haven't seen her.'

'Well, when you do see her, perhaps you can give her this message,' he said. 'Her attempt to use one of my credit cards earlier today has left a trail a mile wide for the authorities to follow. When my wallet was stolen I cancelled all but one of my cards. Of course I lowered the limit available on it, but I wanted to see if she would take the bait and—just like you four years ago—she did.'

Charlotte felt her heart lurch sideways in her chest. Was there to be no end to this torture?

'But of course I am willing to overlook that little indiscretion if you behave yourself,' he added smoothly.

'I can only apologise on my sister's behalf,' she said, shifting her gaze from the steely probe of his. 'She has…some emotional problems and I'm doing my best to help her through them.'

'What sort of emotional problems?'

Charlotte could feel the weight of his gaze as she fixed her eyes on the woodwork of the bar. 'Depression…that sort of thing…our mother died three years ago. She's still missing her terribly.'

Damon signalled for the bartender's attention. He didn't want to have his heart-strings pulled by what was very probably yet another outright lie. As much as he was familiar with grief, he'd seen her sister when she'd propositioned him and she hadn't looked too depressed to him. She'd been bouncy, flirtatious and carefree, her eyes even brighter than her smile.

'What would you like to drink?' he asked again as the bartender approached them.

'Soda water,' she answered without looking at him.

'Nothing stronger?'

'No.'

'You want to keep a clear head so you can keep track of your lies, eh, Charlotte?'

Her eyes flew back to his in a startled glance. 'No… I—I just don't want to drink and drive.'

'You should have caught a cab.'

'I can't afford it.'

'I just gave you a considerable sum of money. Surely you haven't spent it already?'

Not until I get home and book my sister's clinic stay, Charlotte thought with another rush of relief that Stacey was actually going to get clean at last. It would be worth every moment of agony Damon put her through to see her sister put her addiction behind her and develop her full potential, perhaps even return to her studies. Stacey had shown such promise as a young university student. She had topped all of her grades in the science degree she had enrolled in, but it had all come to a grinding halt once she had tasted the compulsive poison of heroin.

'No,' she said into the little silence. 'But it intrigued me when I deposited the cheque as to why you would have an Australian bank account. I don't see why you'd go to that bother if you're only here for a month.'

'I have some business interests here,' he informed her. 'This trip, though short, will not be my last.'

Charlotte nearly choked on her sip of soda water. 'Business interests? *Here?*'

He twirled his brandy for a moment. 'Yes. Apart from my own investment firm in Athens and helping my mother with the Eleni Foundation and the gallery in Oia, I have some investments in an Australian company.'

'What sort of company?' She curled her lip and added, 'Shipping?'

He smiled at her sarcastic expression. 'Now that would be too clichéd, *ne*?'

'I thought all Greek billionaires had an interest in shipping one way or the other,' she said, staring back at the bubbles in her glass.

'I have a yacht, as you may recall from your stay on Santorini,' he said. 'But no, I prefer to keep my investments on solid ground. I have bought a small Queensland island from a private owner. I plan to develop an exclusive Greek-style resort.'

'This is Australia, not Greece,' she reminded him with an arch look. 'Anything you do here will be a cheap imitation of the real thing.'

'It will certainly not be cheap,' he said with a wry smile. 'Not for me in terms of development or indeed for those who wish to stay there once it is completed. It will be a haven for the very rich, no one else need apply.'

Charlotte looked away from his handsome features. When he smiled like that it stirred memories she didn't want stirred. The first thing she had loved about him four years ago had been his smile. It had brightened his eyes with a warmth that had melted her completely—the very same warmth her tiny daughter had exhibited less than an hour and a half ago when her little arms had wrapped around her neck, her soft little mouth pressing loving moist kisses to her cheek.

'Perhaps I will take you there when it is done,' he said, lifting his drink to his lips, his dark eyes still on her.

She blinked at him in alarm. 'You're not serious, surely? I mean…this month…this thing we're…er…doing… it's only for a month, right?'

He tilted his head at her as if eyeing her worth. 'I have been doing some thinking. What if we were to see each other every time I came to Australia?'

Her eyes flashed back at him. 'What if I told you to go to hell?'

He laughed and drained the rest of his drink. 'Then I would have to think of a way of convincing you to change your mind.'

Charlotte put her glass down with a clunk on the bar. 'We agreed on a month and that's all you're getting.'

He placed his empty glass right next to hers, the frosted sides touching. 'Then let's get on with it,' he said and, reaching for her hand, pulled her to her feet.

She had no choice but to follow him. His fingers were like steel around hers, the underlying strength reminding her against going head to head in battle with him, especially in such a public place.

Panic began to claw at her insides. She couldn't do this. Not now. Not ever.

She couldn't sell herself to him.

Not like this.

How on earth did her sister do this with perfect strangers? she wondered sickly. Charlotte at least had loved Damon once…but it still didn't make it right, especially when he had no idea he had fathered a child.

In her escalating dread she considered telling him— perhaps then he would think twice about sleeping with her. But then, she reminded herself, he would think nothing of removing Emily from her custody. He had already demonstrated his ruthlessness; how much more ruthless would he become once he found out he had a child?

The lift arrived with a chiming ping and he ushered her in with a firm hand in the small of her back.

'I—I'm not ready for this,' she said, trying to ease out of his hold. 'It's too soon.'

'It's not soon enough,' he contradicted. 'I should have let you service me in the limousine last night. I was thinking of your dancing little hot breath and flicking tongue all last night. I hardly slept at all.'

His words set off an erotic response in her body she couldn't control. She felt the seeping nectar of need between her thighs and her breasts started to prickle against the lace of her bra.

The lift opened on his floor and he escorted her into his penthouse, closing the door once they were inside with a finality that terrified her.

'Please, Damon…' She struggled to contain her emotions. 'Please give me some time…I'm not…I'm out of practice. I haven't had a lover since… I mean, for a long time…I don't even know if I can…you know…do it any more…'

Damon had to fight his urge to laugh at her paltry attempt to hoodwink him. Hadn't she done this little routine before? The virginal shyness had all been a ruse and he wasn't so foolish as to fall for it a second time.

'I am sure you will quickly recall the necessary steps,' he said. 'You were a fast learner in the past—that is, in fact, if you were indeed learning as you claimed.'

'Please…' Her eyes were bright with moisture. 'Please give me tonight to just talk with you…to get to know you again…before we…do anything else…'

Damon compressed his lips, torn between wanting her and feeling something he didn't want to feel. She was so very beautiful, her skin like smooth cream, her shoulder-length curly chestnut hair like silk, her striking blue eyes luminous and her body a temptation he found hard to resist. She had lost the youthful coltish look she'd had when she'd been in Greece. Her body now at the age of twenty-five, almost twenty-six, was riper, more mature, but, if anything, even more feminine. Her breasts were fuller and her soft curves so alluring he could feel himself hardening just thinking about sinking into her hot slippery warmth.

'You are very convincing,' he conceded. 'But I am not fooled. You are buying time. What do you hope to achieve, Charlotte—another attempt at stealing from me?'

'No, of course not…' It was only as she said the words that she realised how incriminating they sounded. 'I—I mean I didn't steal from you in the first place.'

She could see that he didn't believe her. The suspicion glittered in his eyes as they held hers.

'All right, we will do things your way,' he said with a hard set to his mouth. 'But I am only doing so to see what deceitful little ploy you come up with next.'

'Thank you…' She choked back a sob and rummaged in her bag for a tissue.

He frowned at the relief in her tone. It didn't sit comfortably with him to have her so stricken at the thought of his touch, especially when last night she had responded to him with such heated fervour. He had temporarily unleashed the passionate woman she was, but now she was hiding it from him, shrinking away from him as if she had something to hide…or something else to gain, he reminded himself cynically.

Charlotte blew her nose and, pocketing her tissue, sniffed once or twice to get herself back in control. 'I'm sorry, Damon…this is not what you paid for in terms of company.'

'No, but you and I both know it is only a matter of time before we both get what we want,' he said with arrogant confidence.

Charlotte watched as he moved across the room to pick up the room service menu. It was hard to believe he had given her a reprieve, but for how long? She couldn't hope to hold him off for more than a night or two at the most.

'What would you like to eat?' he asked, handing her the menu.

She looked down at the items without reading a single word. 'I don't know…I'm not very hungry at the moment; why don't you choose?'

He took the menu back from her and reached for the phone by the king-size bed. 'Do you still like seafood?' he asked as he pressed the room service number.

'Yes…I love it…' she answered, privately amazed that he'd remembered that about her. What else had he remembered?

He put an order through and replaced the receiver. 'What about a drink?' he asked. 'The mini-bar is well stocked. Surely one glass of wine won't compromise your driving record?'

But it might compromise my resistance, Charlotte reminded herself. 'No, I'm really happy with soda or mineral water,' she said. 'I have to start early in the morning now that Julian is in hospital.'

'How is your boss, Mr Deverell?'

'He's doing well,' she said. 'I called his wife this afternoon. He came through the angioplasty well but it will be a week or two before he's ready to return to work.'

'He spoke very highly of you,' Damon said, pouring himself a glass of red wine. 'In all of my correspondence with him over the last few months, he has been glowing in his praise.'

Charlotte decided that silence was her best armour.

He turned to look at her. 'I found it hard to believe we were speaking about the same person.'

'I told you before I haven't changed, Damon.'

'No, that is something I am very sure of,' he said, his gaze hardening with bitterness. 'You are still the same person you were when you came to Santorini.'

'I did not steal those sculptures or indeed anything else from your mother.'

'So you keep saying, but you were the only one who could have done so,' he said. 'If you remember, you were given on that day and the ones preceding it, the total responsibility of the gallery. My mother trusted you implicitly. You betrayed that trust.'

'I don't know how that sculpture came to be in my bag, but I swear to God I didn't put it there. As for the other things found in my room at the hostel…' she gnawed at her lip as the memory of that shocking time returned '…I wasn't responsible.'

'Are you forgetting the surveillance cameras we had placed strategically in the gallery?' he asked. 'You were caught on film putting something in your bag on the day in question.'

She blew out a breath of frustration. She had told him all this before. Why wouldn't he believe her?

'I was putting my mobile phone away! My mother had texted me and I heard the phone beeping. I checked my messages but then a customer came into the gallery and I had to wait to put my phone back. That's what you saw on your stupid cameras. Why don't you run a check on the customer? Maybe *they* did it.'

'The customer in question was a tourist from Scotland. I have already done the necessary checks. She is a grandmother from Fife who attends church every Sunday. She didn't steal the statue, Charlotte.'

Charlotte felt her shoulders drop in defeat. There was no way of proving her innocence. It hurt unbearably that he thought her capable of such a betrayal of trust. She had loved working at the gallery; some of the items were so exquisite it had made her feel so privileged to have been left with the responsibility of looking after them. The collection of ancient and modern works Damon's father had gathered over a lifetime had been a wonderful opportunity for her to complete her study of Minoan artefacts. The thought of stealing any item from such an amazing collection was against everything she believed in. She had no idea how and why such precious items had turned up in her bag and in her room. As far as she knew, she'd made no enemies while staying on Santorini; even the two young men at the hostel, although playful and boisterous at times, were the last people she would have expected to show that level of malice. Everyone had been so friendly and welcoming, especially Damon's mother, whom Charlotte had considered a friend virtually from the word go.

'I don't care what you think, Damon. I honoured your mother's trust in me. I would never have betrayed her or you. I was there to do some research for my degree. When I met you in that restaurant that night in Imerovigli I had no idea who you were. At first I thought you were one of the archaeologists working on the Akrotiri site. You seemed to know so much about Minoan artefacts.'

'Which is why you set about charming me, was it not?' he asked. 'You were on a mission. You had a goal in sight and nothing was going to stop you from achieving it. You were systematically removing items from the collection to sell on the black market. It has been done before and much money made out of it. All you had to do was get into my family's good books and your task was made all the easier.'

'I can't make you believe anything other than you want to believe,' she said. 'I know you think I'm guilty, but the only thing I'm guilty of is trusting you too much. I thought we had a solid relationship. I thought that even though we had met and developed strong feelings for each other in a very short time it would be enough to withstand anything. I was wrong.'

He gave her a disgusted look. 'You were not in love with me. You pretended with the skill of an accomplished actor but I know now what wool you pulled over my eyes.'

She looked at him in despair, her voice unable to rise above a distraught whisper. 'You really hate me, don't you, Damon?'

His eyes burned into hers. 'What else do you expect me to feel for you? Love?'

'No…' She lowered her gaze. 'No, of course not…but hating me for something I didn't do is so unjust.'

'It might interest you to know that I was close to falling in love with you four years ago—the closest I had ever been with anyone before or since,' he said. 'I was even prepared to go against the tradition of my family, who had always married within the Greek community, and offer you marriage, but you showed your true colours just in time.'

Charlotte had been well aware of the expectation that he would marry from within his own culture when the time was right. His mother had hinted at it gently from time to time, although she had seemed quite happy for him to indulge his passion with Charlotte and had even at times encouraged it. Alexandrine had told her that a man in his late twenties needed his freedom to prepare for the long road of commitment ahead. Her husband Nicolas had been several years older than her and had enjoyed his playboy lifestyle to the full, finally settling down into the role of devoted husband and father with great happiness and fulfilment until his untimely death when Damon had been a young teenager.

Damon's sister Eleni had been slightly less enthusiastic about Charlotte's affair with her older brother, but to her credit she had still always remained friendly and polite. Charlotte had realised that Eleni was used to having her brother's attention. Since their father's death Damon had been a father figure for her as well as her brother. He clearly adored her and lavished her with attention whenever he could. However, once his affair with Charlotte became more intense, as his sister she'd had to take a back seat in his affections. But, as for her showing any sort of spite, Charlotte had never once seen or heard anything that would make her believe that Eleni was anything other than a lovely young woman who worshipped her older brother.

It was hard to believe that the young girl was now dead. As soon as Charlotte had heard Damon had set up the Eleni Foundation in her memory she had been totally shocked. Eleni Latousakis had been so vibrant, so full of life. It didn't seem possible that she was lying now in a cold grave.

It was equally heartbreaking now to realise that Damon had been close to falling in love with her and had intended to ask her to marry him, but instead she had been accused of theft. She had not even had time to protest her innocence with any degree of conviction as Damon had made it clear she was to leave the island immediately or face the authorities. He hadn't even listened when she had told him she thought she might be pregnant. He had dismissed her callously, claiming he never wanted to see her again and that any child she was expecting couldn't possibly be his. His anger had been monumental and his threats so terrifying that she had decided against going through the harrowing process of facing the police and the deportment authorities. Instead she had boarded the next available flight to Athens and then on to Sydney, her heart shattered and the course of her life changed for ever when the following month it had been confirmed that she had not left empty-handed after all.

She had taken a part of Damon with her…

CHAPTER FIVE

THE room service meal arrived at that moment. Charlotte stood to one side as the trolley was wheeled in, the aroma of their meals luring her appetite out of hiding when the silver lids were lifted after the plates were set down on the table near the windows over-looking the stunning night view of Sydney Harbour.

The attendant bowed out with a generous tip in his hand and Damon moved to pull out Charlotte's chair.

'You are feeling a little hungry now, *ne*?' he asked.

Immensely relieved with the subject change, she freely admitted, 'Yes…a little…'

He took the seat opposite and flicked open his napkin and laid it across his lap. 'You mentioned earlier that your mother died three years ago. Was it sudden?'

'Yes and no…she was ill for a few months, but death is always sudden, even when you're expecting it to occur.' She met his eyes briefly. 'I was so sorry to hear of Eleni's death. That must have been very hard on you and your mother.'

A shadow passed over his face as he reached for his wine. 'It was. It is still hard to believe she is gone.'

'What happened?'

He stared at the red wine in his glass for a moment before he spoke. 'She became tired and run down over a period of several months. She had blood tests taken but nothing showed up. She went to Athens and had a chest X-ray done and it showed lymphoma. She was dead within nine months. The aggressive chemotherapy was supposed to prolong her life. In the end it ended it. She caught pneumonia and slipped away.'

Charlotte felt the prickle of tears for what he must have suffered. His mother Alexandrine would have been devastated, she was sure. Giving birth to her own daughter had made Charlotte realise the depth and breadth of parental love. After all, wasn't that why she was here sitting opposite the man who had fathered Emily so she could protect her, even if it cost her everything she had, including her self-respect?

'I'm so very sorry,' she said again. 'She was a lovely girl.'

'My mother is now very keen for me to marry and have children,' he said, handing her the rocket and roasted kumara salad. 'But so far I have resisted.'

Charlotte took the serving utensils with unsteady fingers, her heart beginning to thump behind her breast. She served a small portion of the salad for herself before asking, 'You don't think it's time for you to settle down?'

He took the bowl from her, his eyes meeting hers. 'I am only thirty-two years old. I would have thought there was plenty of time for me to play the field for a little longer.'

Charlotte couldn't hold his gaze. 'So, like most men, you want to have your cake and eat it too,' she said as she reached for her cutlery.

'What about you, Charlotte?' he asked. 'You are—how old now…almost twenty-six. I would have thought you would have found yourself a rich husband by now.'

'It may surprise you, Damon, but I'm not interested in having a rich husband or indeed any sort of husband.'

'So, like me, you prefer to play the field?'

She frowned. 'No…no, of course not. I hate the shallow

short-term relationships that seem to be so commonplace these days.'

His mouth tilted in cynicism. 'And yet you agreed to this short-term affair with me, did you not?'

She gave him an embittered look. 'You left me with no choice. Do you really think I'd be sitting opposite you now if I'd had any say in the matter?'

Anger flared in his eyes. 'The way I see it, I gave you plenty of choice. You had the choice of seeing your sister arrested or spending time with me, which I might remind you I paid for very dearly. But if you want to put an end to this right now, I will not stop you. You can return my cheque and your sister can face the prosecution she deserves.'

A vision of her sister sitting injecting herself stopped Charlotte from telling him where to put his cheque. She sat stiffly in her chair, her appetite completely gone as the bars of her own prison began to close in on her.

'Nothing to say, Charlotte?'

She brought her fiery gaze back to his. 'I have plenty to say but you've put a lock on my tongue, remember? I have to be polite and charming to you even though you can insult me any time you like. It's hardly what I'd call a level playing field.'

'I would treat you with respect if I thought you were worthy of it,' he clipped out, his mouth tight with anger. 'You betrayed my trust and I will not forget that. The very same lips that kissed mine lied to me time and time again.'

'I have never lied to you.' As soon as she said the words Charlotte felt her colour run up under her skin. Of course she had lied to him! She was lying to him now and felt sure he could sense it.

His eyes narrowed as they clashed with hers. 'You lied to me this evening, Charlotte, and I can prove it.'

His words sent an icy chill down her spine but she forced herself to project an outward calm. 'Oh, really?' she said.

'Yes,' he said, watching her closely. 'You told me you had no idea where your sister was.'

'I don't.'

'I can make one phone call and prove your mendacity.'

She felt her throat begin to tighten in panic, her breath catching in the middle of her chest as she did her best to hold his challenging gaze.

'You see, Charlotte,' he continued, 'I have been keeping a close eye on you.'

Charlotte reassured herself that Emily was safe at Caroline's. She had been for two days in a row. There was no possible way he could know about her existence.

But Stacey was another matter.

She lowered her eyes and accepted defeat, hoping it would keep him away from the truth. 'All right...I admit it,' she said. 'I lied to you about Stacey. She came around to see me this evening.'

'No doubt to share the spoils of her theft with you.'

Her eyes came back to his. 'I had nothing to do with the theft of your wallet.'

'At the very real risk of repeating myself, I am afraid I do not believe you,' he said.

She tossed her napkin aside and got to her feet. 'I'd like to leave.'

His eyes locked on hers. 'You will leave when I give you permission to do so.'

'So, along with blackmail, you're now into abduction as well, are you?' she asked.

'And bondage if it is called for,' he said as he stood up from his chair and, skirting the table, came towards her.

Charlotte started to back away. 'You can't hold me against my will.'

'Ah, but it will not be against your will,' he promised silkily. 'You will be begging to stay, I guarantee it.'

'You promised me you wouldn't do this tonight. You gave me your word.'

He smiled as he came closer. 'So I lied. Doesn't everyone now and again?'

Charlotte felt the back of her knees come up against the huge bed and panicked. 'I can't do this, Damon. I'm not on the pill.'

'I have protection and, if that is not enough insurance for you, then we could always think of other ways to amuse ourselves,' he suggested as his thighs brushed against hers. He took her hand and held it against him, his dark eyes holding hers meaningfully. 'You loved to do so in the past, remember?'

Charlotte could feel the pulse of his body beneath her fingertips and her heart rate began to accelerate. She had to get out of here before she betrayed herself. How could she agree to such an intimate act when he hated her so vehemently?

'I—I can't do this…' Her voice broke on a sob. 'I just can't…' Another sob followed the first, then another until she was crying uncontrollably, her hands going up to her face, her whole body shaking with emotion.

Damon pulled her into his arms and held her close, her shuddering sobs reverberating through his chest. He was shocked by how distressed she sounded. It made him feel as if he had missed something somewhere. He wasn't sure how to handle her in such a state. Had seeing him again brought her guilt back with a vengeance? Perhaps she had tried to put that part of her life to one side and seeing him again had brought it all back.

'Charlotte, do not distress yourself like this,' he said against her fragrant cloud of hair. 'We have done this before, many times in the past.'

She looked up into his eyes, her bottom lip still trembling. 'But not like this…not so cold-bloodedly. Do you have to hate me this much?'

He gave her a rueful smile. 'You think I need to tone it down a bit, *ne*?'

She tried to give him an answering tremulous little smile but it fell a little short of the mark. 'Maybe just a little bit…'

He let out a sigh and brought her back against his chest, his voice rumbling against her breasts. 'Surprising as it may seem, I do not hate you, Charlotte. I desire you. I cannot seem to turn it off, even though I want to.'

Charlotte retreated into the haven of silence.

'You think me a barbarian and a savage for forcing you here but I was prepared to do anything to have you in my arms again,' he went on. 'But I can see you are feeling compromised, as well you should.'

If only he knew how compromised she felt, Charlotte thought.

'So I have come to a decision,' he said, releasing her to look at her upturned face. 'I will give you a couple more days to prepare yourself for our relationship.'

Charlotte blinked at him. 'You mean…I don't have to…'

'No. Not tonight.'

She ran her tongue over her dry lips, her emotions see-sawing between disappointment and relief. She couldn't understand her reaction to his offer of a short reprieve. It wasn't as if she still loved him. He had killed those feelings with his ruthless treatment of her in the past, but still…

She caught her bottom lip with her teeth. 'But you paid me to be your partner for this evening…'

'I have not forgotten our deal,' he said. 'I am just allowing you some breathing space.'

'I'll pay it back.' Charlotte didn't know how she would do it, but she determined she would definitely pay it back.

'Yes, indeed you will,' he said with chilling implacability. 'I want you and I am prepared to wait a day or two until you are ready to come to me willingly.'

She stood uncertainly before him, torn between wanting to bolt and to stay and feel the magic of his touch once more.

She twisted her hands together. 'Damon…I don't know what to say…'

'What I would like you to say is that you will have lunch with me tomorrow,' he said.

She shifted from one foot to the other. 'Um…'

'You do have a lunch hour, do you not?'

'Yes, but I don't think…'

'Just lunch, Charlotte,' he said. 'Nothing else. For now.'

For now.

Charlotte suppressed a tiny shiver as the ominous sound of those two little words seared her soul. She couldn't help feeling that he was toying with her, allowing her to briefly glimpse freedom before snatching it away again. Being with him in any context was flirting with danger. She considered rejecting his invitation but was worried that by doing so he would withdraw his temporary reprieve and insist on her staying this evening.

She couldn't risk it.

But lunch would certainly be a whole lot easier than dinner, she reasoned. Emily would be at crèche all day, which meant she wouldn't have to call upon Caroline to babysit.

'All right…' she said after a little silence. 'Lunch will be fine.'

'I will meet you on the steps of the museum at one p.m. Is that convenient?'

'Yes…' She swallowed the uneven lump in her throat and met his eyes once more. 'So…so you're not going to withdraw your sponsorship for the exhibition?'

His coal-black eyes held no trace of the warmth she craved. 'I am still thinking about it, Charlotte. It depends on many things.'

Her teeth worried her lip again. 'Wh-what sort of things?'

He studied her for a seemingly endless interval.

'I am still making up my mind about you,' he said. 'Whatever you might have done in the past, it seems reasonable to conclude you would not be in such a responsible position now if you had not proven yourself to be trustworthy.'

Hope brightened her eyes. 'So you finally believe me when I say I didn't steal those things from your mother's gallery?'

He took another long moment to answer, his gaze holding hers as if he was still weighing up the pros and cons of her innocence.

'As I told you earlier, I have not yet made up my mind.'

It wasn't quite the answer she was hoping for, but she knew it would have to suffice. There was no way of proving her innocence and the only way forward was to let it go. It was a black mark against her name but it seemed there was nothing she could do to remove it.

Her heart gave a little flutter as his firm warm fingers enveloped hers, his eyes growing even darker as they meshed with her blue ones. He drew her closer to him, his chest brushing against her breasts, his mouth so near hers that his warm breath felt like a caress on her up-tilted face.

'Your mouth is still the most kissable mouth I have ever seen,' he said, his voice low and deep. 'I have thought of it many times over the years.'

'Y-you have?'

'Yes,' he breathed his answer into her mouth as she opened it on a shaky little sigh.

His lips connected with hers in a kiss as soft as feather down, but it was enough to set fire to her soul. She felt the rush of need like a river of flame along her nerve-endings, each one screaming out for more of his touch. His tongue met hers with a flicker of need that sent a shockwave through her entire body. Her breasts came alive as his hands moved up along her ribcage to shape them, her stomach caving in with delight at the feel of his possessive touch. Her mouth was on fire under the onslaught of his, the stroke and glide of his tongue setting her alight with aching need. Her body secretly prepared itself, the deep throb of wanting making her whimper as he began to suckle on her bottom lip. She felt the sexy rasp of his tongue against hers and the scrape of his teeth as his kiss became more and more urgent. His tongue drove into the warm cave of her mouth again and again, reminding her of all the times he had driven into her with his hardened arousal, the thickness of his desire sending her senses on a rollercoaster ride of ecstasy.

How she had missed this wild abandoned excitement. Her body felt alive with sizzling sexual energy, each nerve within her tingling with fully charged responses to his touch.

He broke the kiss to look down at her with desire still burning in his eyes. 'This is probably a good time to stop,' he said with a wry curve to his mouth.

'Yes…yes…I guess it is…'

He took her hands in his. 'Where did you park your car—in the hotel car park downstairs?'

'No…I parked a few streets away.'

'Then I will walk you to it,' he said.

Charlotte's heart gave a sudden lurch. Emily's child booster seat was in the back of her car. 'No!' she said.

He frowned at her emphatic response. 'No?'

'I—I lied…' She reluctantly brought her gaze back to his. 'I didn't drive here tonight…I…I caught a cab.'

His dark gaze studied her for a lengthy pause.

'Why did you feel it was necessary to lie about something as common as catching a cab?' he asked.

'I—I don't know...' she faltered.

His expression closed over as he took her hand. 'Come on, Charlotte. I will escort you to the cab rank.'

She tried to pull her hand away. 'There's really no need to bother.'

His fingers tightened a mere fraction. 'It is no bother, really,' he insisted.

Charlotte had no choice but to allow him to escort her downstairs and into one of the waiting cabs. She gritted her teeth behind her forced smile as he waved her off.

'Where to, miss?' the cab driver asked as he began to pull out of the hotel driveway.

She gave him a sheepish look. 'You're not going to believe this...'

'The airport?' he asked with a grin. 'Every person I've picked up this evening's been going to the airport.'

'Actually, no, much closer than that,' she said with rising colour. 'See that yellow car parked under that tree on the next block?'

'You're kidding me.'

'Sorry.' She grimaced. 'But do you think we can do a few rounds of the block. I don't want my...er...friend to see me getting into my car.'

He gave her another smile. 'No trouble. How many rounds do you think we should do?'

Charlotte glanced back over her shoulder at the hotel, but there was no sign of Damon watching.

'Two should do it,' she said, releasing a sigh as she settled back into the seat.

'Two it is,' the driver said, and made a turn to the left.

* * *

'Stacey?' Charlotte called out as soon as she got back to the flat. 'I'm home.'

A chill ran down her spine when there was no answer. She dropped her bag and called out again, but the flat was eerily quiet.

She checked each of the rooms but it wasn't until she got to her bedroom that she saw the note stuck on her laptop computer screen.

Sorry, Charlie. I know you're going to hate me but I'm just not ready. Forgive me. S.

Charlotte peeled off the note with a sinking heart, the sharp edges of the paper sticking into the soft skin of her palm. She tossed it in the bin but the movement of her hand against her little desk disturbed the computer mouse and the computer screen came to life.

She stared at her internet banking details, her stomach churning in despair when she realised what her sister had done.

'Oh, Stacey…' she cried out in frustration. *'How could you do this to me?'*

CHAPTER SIX

'YOU look nice today,' Diane said as she ran into Charlotte in the ladies' room the following day. 'Are you going out to lunch?'

Charlotte recapped her lipstick and rolled her lips together before answering. 'Yes, I am actually.'

'The Greek billionaire?' Diane guessed with a knowing smile.

Charlotte frowned as she turned to face her colleague. 'You haven't been talking to him, have you?'

'No, why?'

'Listen, Diane.' She lowered her voice conspiratorially. 'Remember we discussed the other evening how Mr Latousakis and I had met before?'

'Yes, on Santorini, right?'

'Well…it's really important you don't talk to him about me. I don't want him to know I'm a single mother.'

'You think he'll be put off if he knows you've got a little kid?' Diane asked.

'You know what men are like these days,' Charlotte said, turning back to the mirror to inspect her make-up rather than meet her colleague's eyes.

Diane gave a deep sigh of agreement as she leaned against the basin. 'Tell me about it. What is it with men and commitment?'

'Exactly,' Charlotte said, relieved she didn't have to go into lengthy explanations.

Diane gave her a probing look. 'He's not Emily's father, is he?'

'No.' Charlotte felt like kicking herself for answering so quickly when she saw the way her colleague's brows rose above her eyes.

Diane pursed her mouth thoughtfully. 'So you're just doing lunch?'

'Yes, just lunch.'

'Does he want to see you again?'

'Maybe…I'm not sure…' Charlotte comforted herself that it was at least the truth. She had no idea what Damon wanted from her. She couldn't quite believe he had temporarily freed her from his previous demands, but for some reason she still felt compromised. She knew it was incredibly dangerous being around him but she couldn't seem to help herself.

She was becoming addicted to his smile, not to mention that kiss…

'But what do *you* want?' Diane asked, as if tapping into her thoughts. 'You said you were involved with him before. Do you still feel anything for him?'

'I can't afford to feel anything for him,' Charlotte answered. 'I have a child and he's a playboy. The two don't go together.'

'You know you could always just tell him about Emily and see what happens,' Diane suggested.

'No. He's only going to be here for a month.'

'What if he finds out some other way? Won't he think you're a bit weird, keeping it from him?'

'He won't find out,' Charlotte said as she straightened her skirt over her hips, wishing she was feeling as confident as she sounded. 'I'm going to make sure of it.'

Diane pushed herself away from the basin. 'Well, for a start you'd better take all those photos of your daughter off the desk in your office,' she advised. 'Damon Latousakis might not be Emily's father, but he sure as hell looks like he could be. Even if he doesn't see the likeness, others certainly will.'

Charlotte stared at her reflection once the door had closed on Diane's exit, the panic in her eyes widening them to the size of dinner plates.

If Diane was already suspicious, what hope did she have with anyone else, including Damon himself?

He was waiting for her when she came out of the museum a short time later and her heart gave a little kick in her chest at the sight of him dressed in a charcoal-grey suit, the crisp white of his shirt highlighting the olive tone of his skin.

He gave her a smile as he looked down at her. 'Hello, Charlotte.'

She returned his smile with a shy one of her own. 'Hello…'

His finger under her chin brought her wandering gaze back to the dark intensity of his. 'Have you forgotten my name?' he asked.

'No, of course not…'

'Say it, Charlotte.'

She felt her stomach give a little quiver. 'Damon…'

His mouth tipped upwards in a satisfied smile as his hand fell away. 'I like the way you say my name. No one else says it quite the way you do. You sort of breathe it out of your mouth in a husky little whisper.'

Charlotte could feel the heat seeping into her cheeks and looked away again. 'We'd better get going; I've only got an hour and with Julian still off sick I've got extra work to do.'

She fell into step beside him as they walked across Hyde

Park, her heart racing each time his arm brushed against hers. Her fingers itched to slip into the warmth of his hand and, to stop herself from being tempted, she crossed her arms over her chest.

'Are you cold?' Damon asked.

'No.'

'Here, take my jacket.' He slipped it from his shoulders and draped it around her. 'The wind is chilly. I heard there is going to be snow on the Blue Mountains this evening.'

Charlotte felt her insides twist as she thought of the clinic Stacey should have been in by now. She had lain awake for most of the night, imagining her sister shooting up all of Damon's money. She didn't want to give up on her own flesh and blood, but she was starting to realise that Stacey—like their father—was fast moving past the point of no return.

'Feeling better?' Damon asked.

Charlotte could barely look at him for the guilt she was feeling. 'Yes…thank you…' She huddled into his jacket, breathing in his scent as the lingering warmth of his body on the expensive fabric encompassed her slim frame.

The restaurant was busy but the *maître d'* escorted them to a quiet table in one corner.

Charlotte examined the menu, hoping it would stimulate her appetite, but every time she saw the price of a meal she was reminded of how empty all of her accounts now were.

'You look worried,' Damon observed. 'What's wrong?'

'Nothing.'

He smiled at her too rapid response. 'Yes, there is; I can see it on your face. I said it was just lunch, OK? No strings. I will even let you pay half if that makes you feel more comfortable.'

'No!…er…I mean, that's not the problem…'

He leaned forward slightly. 'What *is* the problem?'

'I'm just finding this…a little difficult…'

'You and me?'

Her eyes met his briefly. 'Yes…we haven't seen each other in almost four years…I don't know what to say to you…'

'Tell me about your life,' he said, leaning back as the waiter placed water and bread rolls on the table.

'My life?'

He gave her an ironic look. 'You do have one, do you not?'

She looked down at the table. 'I'm sure it's pretty boring compared to yours.'

'What about relationships?' he asked. 'Do you have a serious boyfriend?'

'I would hardly have agreed to spend time with you if I had,' she pointed out with a wry glance in his direction.

'You think I am an arrogant bastard, do you not?'

Charlotte saw no reason to spare his feelings. 'Yes.'

'I was surprised at how seeing you again brought it all back.'

'Brought all what back?'

His smile was crooked. 'No one has ever made me feel the way you do.'

'I'm sure you're just saying that.'

He reached for her hand and enclosed it in the warm temptation of his. 'I mean it, Charlotte. I want you as much as I ever did and you want me. I can see it in your eyes every time you look at me. There's a hunger there that tells me no one has been able to satisfy you the way I did.'

She pulled her hand out of his. 'You broke my heart, Damon. I'm not going back into the ring.'

He frowned as he sat back in his seat. 'Come on, Charlotte. You know I had no choice but to believe you were responsible. Every finger of blame pointed to you.'

Bitterness sharpened her gaze as it connected with his. 'You had a choice to believe me but you chose not to.'

He let out a sigh. 'I have agonised over it for the last four years but I keep coming back to the same point—if you did not steal those sculptures, then who did?'

'I don't know, but someone didn't like the fact that you and I were an item. What about your childhood sweetheart, the woman you were expected to marry?'

'Iona Patonis?'

'Yes. She came into the gallery with Eleni a few times. She was a brooding sort, I always thought. She could easily have done it.'

'Iona would never have done something so despicable,' he insisted. 'She is one of the most kind-hearted people I know. She helped nurse my sister for months and she has been a wonderful support to my mother since Eleni died.'

'Then why haven't you married her?' she asked. 'She clearly expected you to.'

He tapped his fingers on the stem of his wineglass for a moment. 'That is a good question.'

'Are you going to answer it?' Charlotte asked after a short silence.

His eyes came back to hers. 'Iona gave up on me a while ago,' he said. 'She married a cousin of mine. I think you might have met him once—Nick Andreakos. I believe she is already expecting their first child.'

Charlotte hoped her surprise wasn't too evident on her face. 'Did you find that hard to cope with?'

He gave a dismissive shrug. 'Not really. If I had married her, it would have been a marriage of convenience in any case.'

'You didn't love her?'

'I loved her in a brother sister sort of way,' he said. 'But there was no spark, if you know what I mean.'

Charlotte knew exactly what he meant. She could feel it now, just by sitting with her knees so close to his. She had only to stretch out her legs and the heat would explode between her thighs.

She looked down at the menu again and tried to concentrate.

'What would you like to eat?' he asked.

She closed the menu again and put it to one side. 'I'll just have the soup of the day.'

'Is that all?'

'I'm not very hungry. Besides, I have to cook a proper meal when I get home, so…'

'So?'

Charlotte inwardly gulped.

'Why do you have to cook when you get home?' he asked. 'You could have a main meal now and just have a snack later.'

'I l-like to cook.'

'What is your speciality?'

She blinked at him vacuously. 'Speciality?'

'Your favourite dish.'

Her eyes fell away from his. 'Um…it's kind of hard to choose…'

'I did not know you were so domesticated,' he commented. 'When we met four years ago you lived on take-aways or frozen meals.'

'I have since learnt the error of my ways,' she said with a strained effort to smile. 'Thank God for celebrity chefs. Cooking is so hip now.'

'Would you cook a meal for me?' he asked.

Her eyes flared in panic. 'Oh, I'm not that good…really…I can just about manage one of those just add chicken and frozen vegetables…'

'It sounds a whole lot better than hotel food,' he said. 'So how about it? What about you cook for me tomorrow night?'

'I'm busy.'

'The night after?'

'I—I don't cook on weekends.'

'Then I will cook for you,' he said. 'I will bring the ingredients to your house and cook a meal that will totally stun you.'

'My kitchen is tiny…and my oven and cook top doesn't work.'

He gave her a narrow-eyed look. 'You do not want me to come to your house, do you?'

'It's not a house, it's just a rented flat and I haven't had time to clean up for weeks.'

'If your goal is to put me off, let me assure you it is doing the very opposite,' he said.

Charlotte could feel the rising panic beating like a drum in her chest. She could ask Caroline to babysit one more time but the flat was full of little kid stuff. It even *smelled* like Emily.

'I'm not sure it's such a good idea that we see each other again,' she said, actively avoiding his eyes.

The small throbbing silence should have warned her he was preparing a lethal comeback.

'You are forgetting our agreement,' he said in a tone that was ridged with steel. 'I have paid for your company and I intend to get my money's worth.'

She raised her worried gaze back to his, desperately trying to find a way out. 'You're here for a short time and I have…I have someone else.'

'You said there was no one in your life at present.'

She forced herself to resist the urge to look away. 'I was lying.'

'You seem to be rather good at that,' he observed.

'I don't want to complicate my life with the past,' she said. 'What we had is over.'

He grasped her hand once more, his long fingers entrapping hers. 'It's *not* over, Charlotte. You know it is not. How can you say it is over when there is this incredible pulse between us? I felt it that first night. As soon as our eyes met across the room, I knew you felt it too.'

'It has to be over. You think I'm a thief.'

'What's in the past is best left there. This is here and now,' he said, his dark gaze intent on hers. 'We have the chance to explore our attraction again. Let us not waste it.'

She shifted her gaze again, her insides twisting in anguish. 'Don't ask this of me, Damon.'

'Are you in love with this other person?'

She let out a wobbly breath. 'It's not that kind of love…'

'What sort of love is it?'

'It's hard to describe.'

'I am sure they will understand if we spend an occasional evening together,' he said. 'You can tell them you are spending time with an old friend.'

She was so tempted—so very tempted.

'I guess a couple of nights here or there would be OK,' she conceded.

Had she *really* said that? What was she thinking? It was madness to dance with such danger.

'When we met the first time around, we rushed headlong into a physical relationship,' he said. 'I guess that was really my fault. I saw you and I wanted you. But who knows? This time around we might become both lovers and friends.'

Charlotte swallowed the scratchy contents of her throat. 'Friends?'

He gave her another spine-loosening smile. 'You find it hard to see me as a friend?'

'No…I'm sure you'd make a very good friend.' *And a deadly enemy*, she reminded herself.

'Let us start by seeing each other on Monday evening,' he suggested. 'How about dinner and some dancing? I'll send a car to pick you up.'

'No.'

One dark brow rose over his eye. 'No?'

'I—I can make my own way,' she said, lowering her eyes once more.

'All right,' he said after a tiny pause. 'Meet me at my hotel at seven.'

'OK…'

He smiled and raised his glass to hers. 'To us being both friends and lovers.'

Her glass didn't quite make the distance to his. 'To being friends,' she said and, hoping she wasn't courting disaster, downed the contents.

CHAPTER SEVEN

'ARE you serious?' Caroline gaped at Charlotte. 'How could your own sister do that to you?'

'I know.' Charlotte sighed sadly as she watched Emily bend down with Janie to watch a bug climb up a stem of grass. 'I still can't quite believe she'd go that far, but I guess that's drugs for you. Our father was exactly the same. One taste and he was lost.'

'I can lend you some money if you're short,' Caroline offered.

'No, I'll be fine. I got paid yesterday, but thanks anyway.'

Caroline gave her hand a squeeze. 'You've never really given up hope on her, have you?'

Charlotte's mouth twisted. 'She's all I have, apart from Emily.'

'But stealing is a crime whether it's your family you've stolen from or not. What if she's taking other people's money to feed her habit?'

'She already has,' Charlotte said, her expression now grim. 'But she couldn't have picked a worse person to steal from.'

'What do you mean?'

She turned to look at her friend. 'Stacey took a man's wallet the other night, but it wasn't just any ordinary everyday sort of man.'

Caroline's eyes widened with intrigue. 'Uh-oh, this is sounding scary. Who was it? Somebody famous?'

'Even worse.'

'Who?'

Charlotte took an uneven breath and said, 'It was Emily's father.'

'Emily's father?' Caroline almost fell off the park bench. 'You mean he's here in Sydney? I thought you said he lived in Greece.'

'He does, but he's here for a month. He's one of the major sponsors for the exhibition. I was going to tell you, but didn't know how to broach the subject.' She let out a despondent breath and continued, 'Stacey gate-crashed my function the other night and of all people happened to choose Damon Latousakis's wallet to steal.'

'Oh, no…' Caroline gave her a concerned look. 'Are you going to tell him about Emily?'

'If you had asked me that a couple of days ago I would have said a resounding no…but now I'm not so sure.'

'Why?'

'I didn't think he deserved to know after the way he treated me back then. He refused to believe me when I told him I suspected I was pregnant. I called him several times when I found out I knew for sure but he hung up on me every time. I tried writing to him but the letters came back unopened. I even emailed him but he must have deleted each one without reading it. But now I can't help feeling I should have tried harder…I gave up after a few weeks but maybe I should have kept in contact until I finally got through to him.'

'Do you think he'll make trouble?'

'He's a billionaire, Caroline. He would only have to lift his little finger to make trouble. He could have a top-notch legal team assembled before I could even say the word custody.'

'Oh, God, this is terrible.'

Charlotte's expression was wry. 'Believe me, it gets worse.'

'How can it get any worse?'

'He wants to see me.'

'You mean like on a date or something?' Caroline asked, then as realisation dawned she added, 'Oh, my God! You went out with him the other night!'

'I had to, Caroline,' she said. 'He practically blackmailed me into it. He knew it was my sister who took his wallet and threatened to press charges if I didn't agree to see him.'

'You should have told me.'

'I'm sorry…I wanted to but I was so upset I couldn't think straight. I thought it best to keep things as quiet as possible. I thought I could handle it better that way, but now…'

'Now?' Caroline probed.

Charlotte checked on the girls before she turned to look back at her friend. 'Damon wants us to spend some time together, as friends.'

'Yeah, well, didn't anyone ever tell you that you can't truly be friends with an ex?' Caroline said. 'There are always issues, the biggest one, of course, being sex.'

'I know and I don't believe him for a moment but I thought if I spent some time with him I might be able to somehow build up enough courage to tell him about Emily. I need to establish trust between us. He still thinks I'm guilty of theft and Stacey certainly hasn't helped my cause, but if I can show him I'm worthy of his trust he might not be so angry when he finds out he has a child.'

'You're going to have to work damned hard to build enough of a bond between you now to deliver that sort of bombshell.'

'I know…' Charlotte felt her stomach quake at the thought.

'But I guess if he fell in love with you, you might be in with a slim chance,' Caroline mused.

'I'm not sure what he feels but I do know he wants to resume our affair. He's been very up front about that.'

'What about you? Do you still have feelings for him?'

Charlotte looked back at her little daughter and sighed. 'I think I hated him for several months after I left Santorini, especially when he stubbornly refused to acknowledge my attempts to contact him. But as soon as Emily was born I've thought about him every day since. I look into her eyes and I see him. And now that I've met him again it's made me realise I've been in denial about my feelings all this time. I don't think I've ever stopped loving him, not for a moment.'

'Then you'd better get him to fall in love with you again and fast,' Caroline advised. 'Otherwise you stand to lose not just your heart but your daughter as well.'

'Can't I come wif you, Mummy?' Emily asked as Charlotte prepared to leave Caroline's house on Monday evening to meet Damon. *'Please?* I'll be berry good.'

'No, not this time, darling.' She bent down to her daughter's level and kissed the tip of her nose. 'You and Janie need an early night.'

'But I'm not tired.' Emily pouted at her.

Charlotte brushed a fingertip underneath her little daughter's dark-as-night eyes. 'You've got shadows bigger than saucers under here.'

'But I miss you.'

Charlotte felt her heart contract. 'I know, baby, but I have to see a special person tonight.'

'Who?' Emily's thumb crept up to her mouth. 'Auntie Stacey?'

'No…someone I knew a long time ago.'

'Is it my daddy?'

Charlotte stared at her daughter speechlessly. How on earth had she guessed?

'I want to see him too,' Emily said. 'Janie sees her daddy lots and lots and he gives her presents and everyfing.'

'I know but Janie's daddy lives nearby. Your daddy lives in another country.'

'Why doesn't he send me a present?'

'Your mummy is going to be late.' Caroline came to her rescue as she wandered past with an armful of folded towels. 'How about you and Janie have a nice warm bath with lots of bubbles?'

Emily's face brightened as she followed Caroline down the hall. 'How many bubbles?'

'Oh, gosh, trillions and trillions.'

Charlotte gave her friend a grateful smile. 'I'll pick up the girls tomorrow from crèche.'

'Have a good time and don't forget to wear something out-rageously sexy,' Caroline said with a little wink as she shouldered open the bathroom door.

As soon as Charlotte opened the door of her flat she knew her sister was inside.

'OK,' she said, shutting the door with a snap. 'Come and face the music. You've really done it this time. I swear to God, Stacey, I could throttle you.'

Stacey slunk out from the bathroom, her hollow face and darkly shadowed eyes sending a shockwave of concern through Charlotte in spite of her bristling anger.

'I'm in trouble…'

'Damn right you are,' Charlotte said, pushing her concern aside. 'How could you do that to me? Stealing from your own sister, for God's sake! How can you do this after what Dad put us all through? Mum gave up all hope because of what he did and now you're doing the very same thing!'

'There are people after me.'

'I assume you mean the police?'

'No…' Stacey folded her stick-thin arms across her sunken chest. 'I owe money to some people…a lot of money. I paid back what I could—that's why I transferred the funds from your account into mine. I'm sorry, but I had no choice. I'm frightened, Charlie. If I don't pay it all back they're going to come after me.'

Charlotte swallowed against her rising fear to stiffen her resolve. 'I can't give you any more money. I want to help you but I don't trust you. For all I know, this could be another ploy of yours to get your hands on more drugs.'

'I don't want any more money from you,' Stacey said. 'I just need to lie low for a few days. Can I stay here? *Please?*'

Charlotte blew out a sigh. She knew she was going to regret it but what other choice was there? 'All right, but you know the rules. No shooting up, no men and no smoking inside. Got that?'

'I'm sorry, Charlie…about the clinic…I really wanted to go, but the dealer was making threats…'

'I'm not even going to waste my time pleading with you to go. I haven't got the money now, in any case.'

'I'll go back on a methadone programme. I promise.'

'I wish I could believe you, I really do, but I haven't got time to even listen to your empty promises. I'm meant to be meeting a friend at seven and here it is a quarter to and I'm not even dressed.'

'Sorry…' Stacey slumped to the sofa and stared down at her hands.

Charlotte could feel her anger melting. 'Try and get some rest and we'll talk in the morning,' she said gently. 'Emily's staying at Caroline's. I might be late, so don't wait up.'

'Is this the same guy as the other night?'

'Yes…but we're just friends.'

Stacey gave a cynical little grunt. 'That's what they all say.'

Damon was waiting for her in the bar when she arrived, flustered and with heightened colour, her chestnut hair half up and half down as if she'd just got out of bed, but somehow on her it looked incredibly sexy, not the least bit messy.

'I'm sorry I'm late,' she said, meeting his eyes briefly. 'It was one of those days.'

'How about a drink to settle your nerves?' he suggested.

She lifted her chin at him. 'I'm not nervous.'

He smiled and watched as the colour in her cheeks delicately spread. He lifted a finger and stroked it along the rosy curve of her face. 'Yes, you are.'

Her mouth twisted ruefully as she slipped on to the bar stool beside him. 'All right, I admit it. I am.'

'You do not need to be nervous, Charlotte,' he said. 'This evening is to re-establish a friendship between us.'

She looked at him with wide uncertain eyes. 'Do you think ex-lovers can ever truly be friends?' she asked.

He looked down at her upturned face, his gaze lingering on the soft bow of her mouth. 'Who knows?' he said, meeting her gaze once more. 'I had every intention of giving it a try, but as soon as you walked in I wanted to take you upstairs and—'

She put a finger up to his lips to stall his speech. 'Don't, please…this is hard enough without you tempting me like that.'

He captured her finger and, bringing it up to his mouth, pressed his lips against it. 'So you are tempted?'

She drew in a husky little breath. 'A bit…'

'Only a little bit?'

Her lips curved upwards in another twisted smile. 'OK, a lot.'

He brought her finger back up to his mouth and sucked on it, his eyes still holding hers.

Charlotte felt the tug of desire between her legs, heat exploding like a burst of fuel-driven flame. How could she have ever thought they could simply be friends? It was impossible with this need pulsing between them. She could feel it in the air as it tightened around them. She could see it in his eyes as his pupils flared and she could feel it in his touch. The touch her body remembered so well it positively ached to feel it again.

'Damon…'

'No.' He used the same tactic she had done to stop her from speaking, his finger making her lips buzz with sensation. 'Listen to me. We have a past that will not go away. I can feel it like a living breathing entity between us.'

'I can't give you what you want.'

'Yes, you can,' he insisted. 'You can relieve me from this torment of longing. We were so good together. We can be so again. I know it. I feel it every time I touch you.'

'Damon…' She took a breath to prepare herself. 'There's something you should know…'

'I know all I need to know,' he said. 'You still want me. We can never be just friends, Charlotte. There is too much passion between us.'

'We can't have a future unless we deal with the past.'

'The past is in the past, Charlotte. I do not want to revisit it again. I believed you to be guilty of a crime you still say you did not commit. I want to believe you are incapable of lying but I think it best that we leave it at that. It bears no relevance to what is between us now.'

Charlotte felt the crushing weight of her guilt press against her chest. She could hardly breathe for the unbearable load of it. She was deceiving him at this very moment.

'This is a second chance for us,' he said. 'I was wrong to

cut off all contact with you. I see that now. It was born out of anger and pride and it served no purpose. I should have listened to your explanation. I owed you that at the very least, but I was too damned proud.'

'Damon…I don't know how to tell you this, but—'

'Do not say you hate me, for I do not believe it,' he said, interrupting her.

'No, I don't hate you, but I…' She swallowed the rest of her words.

'I know you are uneasy about us resuming our relationship,' he said. 'You were hurt before and no doubt still feel vulnerable, but I will try not to rush you, even though it is killing me.'

She gave him a little smile in spite of her anguish. 'You only have two speeds, Damon: fast and faster.'

He grinned at her. 'You know me so well, *agape mou*, even after all this time.'

'Excuse me, Mr Latousakis.' A hotel employee approached them. 'The meal you requested is now ready in your room.'

'Thank you,' Damon said.

Charlotte raised her brows. 'We're eating here? At the hotel?'

He took her hand and helped her from the stool. 'I hope you do not mind. I wanted us to be alone.'

She nervously followed him to the bank of lifts. She had been expecting a public restaurant and a dance floor with other couples, not a private intimate meal in his penthouse suite. Resisting him was going to be a whole lot harder without an audience to restrain her desire to be in his arms again.

He opened the door for her and she stepped in to see fragrant flowers in every corner of the room, candles flickering and a bottle of French champagne sitting in an ice bucket beside the table, which was set for two.

'You've gone to so much trouble…' She looked around her in amazement. 'I don't know what to say…'

He pulled out a chair for her. 'Come and sit down and we will enjoy the meal the chef has prepared specially.'

Heat coiled in her stomach at the look in his eyes as he took the chair opposite. He was so dangerously sexy when he looked at her like that. She had no defences to withstand the temptation of his smile, let alone his touch.

He served their meal from the dishes set on a trolley beside the table, each movement of his hands reminding her of how those long fingers had known every inch of her body.

She had given herself so freely to him. Her lack of experience had not been an issue; she hadn't even mentioned it until after they had made love. Her body had felt no discomfort in receiving him the first time; she had felt as if she had been made for him and him alone.

'You are very quiet,' Damon remarked once their entrée and main meal was over.

'Sorry…I was miles away.'

'I am boring you?'

'No, of course not…it's just that…'

He reached for her hand and held it in the warmth of his. 'Shall we dance?'

'Dance? Here?'

He pulled her to her feet. 'You loved to dance, Charlotte, remember? You always moved in my arms as if we were one person.'

She sent her gaze downwards. 'I haven't danced in years…'

He flicked the switch on a remote control and the soft strains of a romantic ballad filled the air.

She felt his arms come around her and her feet moved in time with his, her body so close to the warmth of his, she felt her heart begin to increase its pace.

'See?' he said, his deep voice a sexy rumble against her breasts. 'You fit so well against me.'

Charlotte gave herself up to the music and the feel of his body moving in time with hers. It was like stepping back in time, her whole body acting as if the past had not happened. Her arms looped around his neck, which brought her even closer to his growing erection. She felt it harden against her and when she looked up into his eyes she knew there was no way she would be able to resist him, audience or not.

His hands were like hot brands on her hips, his muscled thighs moving against and between hers as they moved together until she was almost mad with the need to feel him fill her. She could feel her body seeping with the sensual silk of womanly desire, her nipples tightening in anticipation of his touch as his hands moved from her hips to settle just below her breasts.

His mouth swooped down and covered hers with a searing kiss of passion, his tongue stroking through the parted curtain of her lips in search of hers. She flicked her tongue against his, tentatively at first and then with increasing confidence as she felt the pulse of his reaction. His mouth was a burning pressure on hers, the movement of his hands as they found her breasts making her gasp with pleasure.

'You are wearing too many clothes,' he growled as his fingers found the zip of her dress and slid it downwards.

'So are you,' she said and began to undo the buttons of his shirt, lingering to press a hot little kiss as each part of his chest was exposed.

He groaned when she got to his belt and, lifting her, carried her to the bed, joining her in a tangle of limbs and half-discarded clothes.

Charlotte put her hand over his as he reached for her knickers, which only just covered the seam of her scar. 'Can we turn the lights down?' she asked.

He frowned. 'But I want to see you—all of you.'

'I'm not as slim as I used to be…'

'You look wonderful to me,' he said.

'Please, Damon.'

He reluctantly reached across to dim the lights. 'All right, but next time I want to see every inch of you.'

Charlotte felt the thrill of his urgent arousal as he came back over to her, his hands tearing at her clothes as she tore at his, their bodies straining to join in the most intimate of all embraces. She ached with the need to feel him inside her, the heavy pulse of desire like the beat of a primitive tribal drum, reverberating throughout her body.

His mouth moved to her breast and sucked hard, the rasp of his tongue making her toes curl and her back arch in response. He moved to her other breast, his hands stroking her belly and moving lower until he found the secret heart of her, his fingers stroking into her slippery warmth until she was writhing with pleasure. She felt her body begin to tingle with the first waves of release but it wasn't enough. She reached for him, her fingers shaping his turgid length, his agonised gasp inciting her to increase the pressure until he was struggling to contain control.

He grasped at her hand but she pushed him with her free one until he was on his back, his chest rising and falling as she began to move her mouth from the flat taut plane of his abdomen in teasing little wet kisses until she came to the pulsing heat of him.

He groaned again when she licked at his swollen length, her tongue tasting him before she opened her mouth over the satin-covered steel of his body, drawing him in with stroking and rolling movements of her tongue.

'Enough!'

He pulled her away from him and flipped her on her back, rummaging quickly for a condom and applying it before driving into her with such urgency she cried out in sheer relief that he was finally where she most wanted him. His movements were hard and fast but she was with him all the way, her body rocking against his as it climbed towards the pinnacle of release it craved.

'I am going too fast,' he said breathlessly against her mouth.

'You're not going fast enough.' She urged him on with her body, rising to meet each forward movement of his.

Suddenly she was there.

Her whole body tightened and then exploded, splintering into a thousand tiny pieces, each one of them shivering with the aftershocks of pleasure.

She felt his explosive release hard on the heels of hers, every muscle in his body tensing before he let go with a deep primal groan. They lay still intimately entwined, basking in the afterglow of deep contentment.

Damon eased himself up on his elbows to look down at her. 'I had planned to take things slowly but you made it impossible. Your body excites me like no other.'

'You're pretty exciting too,' she said, reaching up to stroke his jaw with her hand.

He captured her hand and pressed a soft kiss to the middle of her palm. 'Have you had many other lovers since me?' he asked.

'Why do you ask?'

His eyes roved her face, lingering on her mouth before returning to her blue gaze. 'It is selfish and chauvinistic of me, I know, but I was hoping you have not.'

Her expression contained a hint of reproach. 'I'm sure *you* haven't been celibate for the last four years.'

A little frown tugged at his forehead. 'No…'

'Have you been in love with anyone?' she asked, trying to ignore the pain his confession had evoked.

He shook his head. 'No. I have not allowed myself to feel that way about anyone.'

Charlotte felt hope begin to rise in her chest. Did he still feel something for her?

His eyes gave nothing away as they connected with hers but she could feel his body thickening inside her.

His hands began to explore her breasts, his thumbs reacquainting themselves with the rock-hard pebbles of her nipples, his hot moist mouth moving down to suckle on each of her breasts until her head was spinning and her ears ringing with the pleasure of having his strong arms around her and his lips and tongue playing havoc with her senses all over again.

Damon pulled away from her breast and looked down at her with a quizzical expression. 'What's that noise?' he asked.

'What noise?' she asked dizzily, her mind still reeling from his sensual onslaught.

'It sounds like a mobile phone on vibrate,' he said.

Charlotte felt her stomach lurch in panic. It was late and the only people who would be calling her at this hour would be either Caroline or Stacey.

'Um…I'd better answer it.'

He looked at her incredulously, his body pulsing with need inside hers. *'Now?'*

'It might be my sister,' she said and eased herself out of his embrace.

She walked on unsteady legs to her evening bag but the phone had stopped vibrating by the time she got to it. She stared at the screen as a message icon appeared. She pressed the key to display the text and her heart came to a stumbling halt when she read what was there.

Emily hurt—but don't worry—have taken her to the Children's hospital—C xox

Charlotte hadn't even noticed that Damon had come to stand beside her until she heard his deep voice ask in a tone that demanded an immediate answer, 'Who is Emily?'

CHAPTER EIGHT

'I—I HAVE to go…' Charlotte almost fell over her feet to get to her clothes, struggling back into them with jerky agitated movements. 'I have to go *now*…'

'Who is Emily?' Damon asked again, this time restraining her by the arm.

She looked up at him in desperation as she tugged her arm out of his hold. 'She's…she's my daughter; now please let me go—I have to go to the hospital. *Oh, God!*' She began to cry as her keys dropped out of her grasp. 'This is all my fault. I knew something like this would happen. It's all my fault.'

'Your daughter?' Damon stared at her in stupefaction. *'You have a child? You really have a child?'*

She nodded as she scooped up her keys, tears running down her cheeks. 'I was going to tell you…I just didn't know how to go about it.'

His frown was so heavy his brows met over his eyes. 'You agreed to have a relationship with me while you are married with a child?' He looked at her incredulously. 'What sort of woman are you?'

She brushed at her eyes and said, 'I'm not married…'

'Where is the child's father?'

She bit her lip. She couldn't tell him like this. 'I have to go, Damon. We can talk some other time. *Please.*'

'You are in no fit state to drive,' he said, reaching for his coat. 'Give me your keys. I will take you.'

'No, you don't know your way around the city and I'll be much quicker on my own.'

He took her arm again and this time there was no hope of escaping. 'Then we will go by cab, which will be even quicker. You will not have to worry about parking.'

It made good sense to Charlotte, although she knew there would be a price to pay for accepting his help. But she was beyond caring. She had to get to the hospital to see what was wrong with Emily.

Guilt struck at her from every angle. She should never have left her daughter tonight. For days now Emily had seemed unusually clingy, but she'd put it down to her being over-tired. And now her little girl was in hospital, all because of *her* neglect.

The cab trip was mercifully swift but, although Charlotte did her best to resist any attempts at conversation with Damon, he was not so easily put off.

'Shouldn't you be contacting her father?' he asked.

She huddled herself into the corner of the cab. 'No.'

'What do you mean, no? Surely her father should know of this emergency?'

'He doesn't even know she exists.'

He stared across at her in the semi-darkness of the cab's interior. 'What do you mean, he does not know? Why have you not told him? Surely every man, no matter what the circumstances, has the right to know he has fathered a child.'

She gave him a resigned look, as if the world had finally caught up with all of her frantic attempts to escape from it. 'Actually, I did tell him but he chose not to believe me.'

Damon felt as if someone had just struck him in the chest with a blunt object. Surely it couldn't be true?

It wasn't possible.

A niggling doubt crept into his mind, like a curl of smoke finding its way under a locked door. He had thought she'd been lying to save her pride, but what if he'd got it wrong?

They had used protection, he reminded himself. But the doubt tapped him on the shoulder again as he recalled those last few times before he had sent her away...

His passion for her had been uncontrollable. He had surged into her warmth, relishing the intoxicating experience of feeling her silk against his steely strength without a barrier.

'I'm her father?' he croaked.

She answered him with a tiny nod.

'I do not believe you.' He regretted the words as soon as they left his lips but there was no way he could take them back. He saw the way they wounded her, the hunch of her shoulders as if protecting herself from further pain, the stiffness of her limbs and the set of her mouth making him realise how hard she was trying to cope.

'Well, that's to be expected, of course,' she said with bitterness sharpening every word to a dagger-point. 'You have never believed me before, so I don't expect you to do so now.'

He finally found his voice, although it didn't really sound like his when he finally spoke. 'Why did you not tell me?'

Her blue eyes were brimful of resentment. 'I did tell you, but you refused to accept the possibility that I was carrying your child. You accused me of theft. It was clear from what you said that you thought I was lying to get you to do something you weren't prepared to do, like give my child a name—your name.'

The cold hard vice of guilt pressed against him. He felt it in every part of his body. His chest felt so constricted he could hardly breathe and his stomach was churning with a nauseating dread that he had somehow got it wrong.

He had sent her packing with the threat of exposure and immediate deportation. He had been so convinced of her guilt that he hadn't even bothered to look for another suspect.

But there were no other suspects, he reminded himself, not unless he was prepared to lay the blame at his mother or sister's feet.

But what if Charlotte had planned this? A few sculptures were nothing compared to this. As revenges went this was surely up there with the best. She had kept his child from him all this time, not once trying to resume contact after those first few times.

'I have a daughter…' The words felt strange on his lips, like a language he had never learned to speak but, to his surprise, was now suddenly fluent in it.

'I called her Emily Alexandrine,' she said into the taut silence.

He swivelled his tortured gaze back to hers. 'You gave her the name of my mother?'

Her eyes were still shining with tears. 'I thought it was the least I could do. Your mother had been so kind to me in offering me a job at the gallery…'

Damon turned away to look at the glittering lights of the highway as the cab made its way to the hospital he could see in the near distance, his throat closing over with pain.

His daughter was within the structures of that concrete and glass building. A daughter he had never realised existed until this moment, a daughter who connected him with Charlotte in the most intimate way possible, the combination of their blood flowing through her tiny veins.

'How old is she?' he asked, his voice sounding hollow.

'She turned three years old three months ago—her birthday is the fifteenth of April.'

Damon closed his eyes against the rush of emotion her

words evoked. He had missed out on *so* much. Her entire babyhood had gone and he hadn't seen a thing. She would be walking and talking and yet he had never held her as an infant, had never changed her nappy, had never seen her first smile or first tooth or first anything. He could have walked past her on the street and would never have known she was his child.

'How could you have done this to me?' His words fell into the silence like a solid weight against a fragile glass surface.

Charlotte flinched beside him. 'I had no choice. You believed me to be a thief. You sent me packing with your threats ringing in my ears. I tried to tell you so many times.'

His eyes met hers in the subdued lighting of the cab as it pulled into the emergency bay of the hospital. 'But you are a thief, Charlotte.' His voice was tight with anger, each word hardbitten. 'You have stolen from me my daughter and I swear to God you will not get away with it this time. I let you off lightly when you betrayed my family's trust the last time, but not now. A few ancient sculptures are nothing to the value of my own flesh and blood. You will regret not telling me of my child's existence—I guarantee it.'

Charlotte stumbled from the cab with his words reverberating in her pain-racked body as she made her way to the reception desk to find out where her daughter was being held. She had tried Caroline's mobile in the cab but it had frustratingly gone to message service each time.

'Emily Woodruff?' The hospital receptionist looked through the long list of patients on her computer. 'I'm sorry, but there's no patient of that name who has been admitted up until the last hour. Have you tried Accident and Emergency? She might still be being assessed.'

Damon took Charlotte's elbow as they made their way through the endlessly long corridors to the Accident and Emergency bay on the ground floor.

Charlotte pressed the security button and quickly explained the situation to the receptionist who appeared at the window.

'Oh, yes, the little girl—she's being assessed right now,' the woman said, releasing the door. 'Come on through.'

There were numerous curtained cubicles with a variety of people moving in and out of them, nurses and doctors and worried-looking relatives adding to the general sense of urgency and despair of the place.

'Excuse me…' Charlotte began as a doctor rushed past.

'I need a chest drain in Emergency One, stat,' the harried doctor said to a nurse before turning to Charlotte. 'Could you please wait in the waiting room? Someone will attend to you shortly.'

Damon stepped forward. 'Our daughter has been admitted to this hospital and we would like to know where she is.'

The doctor stopped in his tracks at the authority in Damon's tone. 'You must be little Emily Woodruff's parents. I'm sorry—we've been so busy this evening. She's just been taken down to X-ray.'

'What's wrong with her?' Charlotte asked, panic beating like the wings of a startled bird in her chest.

The doctor gave them both a reassuring smile. 'Nothing too serious. It looks like a greenstick fracture to her arm. It won't even need plaster. The X-ray is just to confirm my diagnosis. The young woman who brought her in is in Emergency Bay five.'

Caroline must have heard their voices as she was already coming out of the cubicle with Janie half asleep in her arms.

'Oh, Charlotte, I'm so sorry. It happened so quickly. I was on the phone to my mother. The girls really should have been in bed but they were playing so happily and I wasn't watching for a moment and Emily fell off the sofa. I'm so sorry. I don't know what to say…'

'It's all right.' Charlotte gave her a quick hug, careful not to disturb little Janie. 'The doctor said it's just a greenstick fracture.'

'It *is* serious,' Damon said with a glaring frown. 'What sort of babysitter allows a small child to injure herself?'

'Damon, please…' Charlotte put a hand on his arm. 'This is not the time to—'

'Not the time to what?' he said, interrupting her coldly. 'To tell me what I should have been told nearly four years ago? That is my daughter in there and I want to know how she came to be injured.'

'You're Emily's father?' Caroline said somewhat unnecessarily.

Charlotte's eyes closed, her fingers coming up to pinch the bridge of her nose as the tension of the evening built to explosion point in the middle of her forehead.

'Yes,' Damon answered stiffly. 'Although I have only been informed of the fact less than fifteen minutes ago. How did my daughter injure herself?'

Charlotte, seeing the distress on her friend's face, stepped forward. 'Damon, please—this is not Caroline's fault. Children hurt themselves all the time. Emily gets clumsy when she's tired and falling off a sofa is virtually an everyday occurrence in a child of three. It's not fair to blame Caroline.'

Damon turned his glittering gaze on her. 'So it is you I should blame, is it not? For you are her mother and you left her under inadequate supervision.'

Anger flared in her eyes and, even though she knew it was unfair to dump what was really her own guilt on him, she did so regardless. 'You were the one who insisted I spend this evening with you. If I hadn't been forced to be with you, this might never have happened.'

Damon opened his mouth to defend himself when the rattle

of a trolley turned his head and he saw his little daughter for the very first time…

'Mummy?' Emily's little voice was strained and fearful as her chocolate-brown eyes went to where Charlotte was standing beside Caroline.

'Oh, precious…' Charlotte rushed to her and kissed her gently on her forehead, both her cheeks and the tip of her tiny nose. 'Are you all right, darling? The doctor said you hurt your arm. You're being so brave. Does it hurt very much?'

Emily's bottom lip wobbled precariously. 'Not now…I just wanted you to be wif me…' She began to cry, big tears popping out of her eyes like oversized crystals.

Damon swallowed the rising emotion in his throat. He felt shut out and isolated. His own flesh and blood didn't even recognise him, although he could see without a doubt she was his child. He had considered demanding a paternity test but he could see now it would be pointless. Emily looked exactly as Eleni had looked at the same age—the same dark brown, almost black hair, the same bottomless brown eyes and the same rosebud mouth and button nose.

Pain twisted inside him like a trapped and angry serpent, the venom of his anger stinging him in every possible place.

He had a child—a little daughter that Charlotte had kept from him. In spite of his earlier refusal to believe her, she'd had almost four years to tell him and yet she hadn't. She hadn't even told him over the last few days and yet she'd had every possible chance to do so. Three of his daughter's birthdays had already passed; what else would he have missed if he hadn't found out?

'Ms Woodruff?' The doctor who had spoken to Charlotte earlier came over with an envelope containing Emily's X-rays. 'Your daughter is free to go home. It is, as I suspected, a greenstick fracture, which requires nothing but a firm bandage and a review by an orthopaedic surgeon in three weeks. Here is a list of names of orthopaedic surgeons—you can choose one of these or go to your GP and they will refer you to one.' He turned to his little patient with a smile. 'You were very brave, Emily. I had a ten-year-old boy in here the other night with exactly the same condition and he yelled the place down.'

Emily's big brown eyes went wide. 'Weally?'

He gave her hair a quick but gentle ruffle. 'I didn't just have to bandage his arm—I was tempted to put a big plaster over his mouth.'

Emily giggled.

'Thank you so much, Dr McHenry,' Charlotte said after a quick glance at his name tag. 'I'm so sorry I wasn't here with her when she came in.'

The doctor gave her a tired smile. 'I'm a parent myself,' he said. 'My wife and I both work shifts, so I know what a juggle it is with childcare and babysitting. Your friend did the right thing in bringing Emily in so promptly. Now, if you'll excuse me, I must see to the rest of my patients. I'll send a nurse over to see to that bandage. I even think we've got a pink one especially for little girls. Good luck, Emily, and don't go falling off the sofa any more.'

'I won't.' Emily smiled shyly.

Charlotte stood to one side as the nurse gently and expertly bandaged her daughter's arm.

Caroline had quietly excused herself just moments before with Janie fast asleep on her shoulder, but Damon was still standing watching her with a stony expression on his face and Charlotte knew without a doubt that her nightmare of a night was far from over…

CHAPTER NINE

EMILY was asleep almost before the cab arrived, her little dark head lolling against Charlotte's shoulder as she walked to the hospital entrance with Damon at her elbow.

She could feel his simmering anger; it was almost palpable in the cold night air. It was coming off him in scorching waves that threatened to peel off her skin every time he looked at her.

'You have a lot of explaining to do,' he bit out as he waved down a cab.

'This is not the time or place,' she said. 'I need to get Emily home and into bed.'

'This is not over, Charlotte,' he warned her. 'I swear to God this is not over.'

The cab arriving forestalled any further speech and Charlotte sank into the seat with her daughter snuggling up close.

'Put her in the seat belt,' Damon instructed.

Charlotte's blue eyes battled with his for a moment before she did as he demanded, even though it produced a whimper of pain from Emily. She hadn't wanted to let her daughter go even for a second, but she knew he was right. Even a short journey could be dangerous without the protection of a seat belt.

Damon leaned forward to give the cab driver directions and

Charlotte felt her heart give a tiny flutter. He had very definitely had tabs on her if he knew where she lived.

She sat back in her seat with Emily's dark head on her lap, wondering how he would view her tiny run-down inner city rented flat. It was all she could afford. Childcare cut into her budget and, with Stacey's ongoing demands, she often sailed a little too close to the wind. There were few luxuries. Some weeks it was all she could do to keep food on the table.

'I cannot believe you have kept this from me for all this time,' he inserted into the stiff silence.

'If you remember, I did tell you,' she threw back. 'But you refused to believe me. I tried phoning and emailing you, but you blocked all contact.'

'You could have told me the first night I saw you at the museum! She's *my* child!' He glared at her furiously. 'Do you have any idea of how much I have missed out on? *Do you?*'

Her eyes flashed at his, her tone unmistakably sarcastic. 'So this is now all about you, is it, Damon? I'm sorry, but I thought it was about a little child who has suffered an injury. Pardon me for being so remiss in putting her needs over yours.'

His jaw tightened until she could see white tips at the edges of his mouth. 'I should have been told. As soon as I saw you the other night, you should have told me.'

She sent him an embittered glance. 'I would have told you if I hadn't thought you would whip her away from me as soon as she was born.'

There was a deadly little pause.

'I can still do that.'

Charlotte's eyes flew back to his, her heart threatening to jump out of her chest. 'You can't do that! She's my daughter.'

His eyes were like black diamonds. 'She is my daughter as well. And, from what I have seen so far, you are not looking after her with any degree of competency.'

'That's not true!'

He gave her a cynical look. 'How can you possibly say that when she is lying between us with a serious injury?'

'She hurt her arm,' Charlotte said. 'It's not the least bit life-threatening. Children hurt themselves all the time. It could have happened at crèche.'

His eyes burned with fury. 'You send her to crèche to be looked after by strangers?'

She rolled her eyes at him. 'I'm a single mother, Damon, and just like any other single mother I have to work to put food on the table. And, as much as I would love to be with Emily full-time, I don't have the luxury of that choice, so yes—I do allow strangers to look after her, but they are highly qualified strangers who each have a fully accredited childcare certificate.'

'You will withdraw her from care immediately.'

Charlotte tightened her mouth. 'I will do no such thing.'

'You will cancel her childcare arrangements, for from now on you will be a full-time mother to her.'

'I have a job!' she reminded him heatedly. 'I have commitments regarding the exhibition.'

'Cancel them.'

'I can't cancel them! Julian is out of action and it's all up to me to pull this off. I can't pull out now, even if I wanted to.'

'I will withdraw my sponsorship if you do not quit your job. I will also tell your employers of your history of theft. I was starting to believe you were innocent, but I can see now you were not. You have no trouble with lying; it comes to you so naturally.'

Charlotte felt the tension building to breaking-point. She could barely see for the white spots of it disturbing the line of her vision. She felt sick with dread in case he did as he threatened. He had so much power and she had so little...

'Please...' She turned to look at him, her eyes awash with

unshed tears. 'I know you are angry and I can understand how you must feel, but you will be hurting your daughter if you hurt me. I have only ever acted in her best interests. You have to believe that. I had no choice over seeing you again because you saw me as a thief. Do you know how many times I wished I could have picked up the phone in the last three years and told you of her existence? I wanted to every day of her life but I couldn't. You made it impossible for me by labelling me the way you did. You shut me out of your life. You charged me with a crime I did not commit.'

'You lie!' He threw the words at her like stinging arrows. 'You are lying now. You were never going to tell me of my daughter's existence. I know that. I can see it in your eyes. You wanted this last hold of power over me. The ultimate revenge was to have stolen the most priceless thing of all—my child.'

Charlotte set her mouth. 'I did *not* steal her,' she said. 'You threw her away when you threw me away.'

'When did you suspect you were pregnant?'

'I was late and started to worry. I know condoms aren't foolproof and although I'd gone on the pill I wasn't sure it had kicked in when…when we…' She moistened her dry mouth and continued, 'When you came to the gallery that afternoon I tried to tell you of my suspicions, but you had suspicions of your own.'

Damon struggled to listen without interrupting. He wanted to defend his actions but he was starting to see that Charlotte had been in a difficult situation.

'I didn't have the pregnancy confirmed until I was back in Sydney,' she said in a subdued tone, her fingers brushing back the silky hair off Emily's peacefully sleeping face.

Another tense silence tightened the air between them.

'Was it deliberate?' he asked. 'As a way of snaring yourself a billionaire?'

She sent him a furious glance. 'How can you ask that? I

was halfway through my Honours degree. I had a chance to sidestep a Masters to have a go at a Ph.D. Why would I deliberately compromise that by getting pregnant on purpose? And, if I had, why then would I keep it a secret for all this time?'

Damon turned his head to look out at the city streets flashing by. It was raining, the cold sheets of icy moisture reminding him of how far away he was from home. He felt out of his depth, not just because of the climate change but because everything had changed.

He was a father.

He had responsibilities he had to face, even though the thought of tying himself to a woman who had exploited him and his family was anathema to him.

Yes, he still desired her. She was a fever beating in his blood and the fact that she had borne his child only made it a thousand times worse. They were connected in the most intimate way possible, their blood lines linked, their future enmeshed in the body of the small, exquisitely beautiful child lying between them.

He knew his mother would be beside herself with joy to find she had a grandchild, especially so soon after the tragic loss of Eleni. How much hurt would little Emily repair by meeting her grandmother for the first time?

'Once the exhibition is over we will go to Santorini,' he said.

Charlotte stared at him in shock. 'I'm not going anywhere with you.'

His eyes met hers with a challenge she knew was going to be hard to withstand. 'You come with me, Charlotte, or I swear to God you will never see your daughter again.'

She swallowed convulsively. 'You can't do that…'

His expression was unmoved by her emotionally charged statement. 'I can and I will. You have reared my child in an unsafe environment. She is daily exposed to danger. Tonight is a case in point. God knows what we will find at your flat.'

Charlotte felt her heart sink in despair. Stacey wasn't to be trusted. She sat on the edge of her seat, the sharp teeth of terror gnawing at her insides as the cab driver pulled into her street…

The bedroom light was on in her flat, which hopefully meant Stacey had taken her up on her offer of a bed for the night.

Damon had Emily in his arms, his hold so gentle and protective it brought tears to Charlotte's eyes as she led the way to the door.

She heard a low male groan as soon as she opened the door, her heart instantly tripping in alarm.

'Come on, baby, give it to me,' the stranger's voice said. 'I paid you double the money—now deliver.'

Charlotte shut the door with a snap and turned to face Damon's thunderous frown, her back pressed flat against the door. 'W-we can't go in there…'

His jaw tightened until she could see a pulse leaping at the side of his mouth. 'Your sister?' he asked.

The colour of her shame answered for her. 'Yes.'

'How often does this occur?' he asked.

She knew he wouldn't believe her but she felt compelled to defend herself. 'It hasn't happened before, I swear it hasn't.'

She was right—he didn't believe her. His disgust was evident on his face as he made his way back to the pavement with Emily still asleep in his arms.

'Damon…' Charlotte rushed after him. 'I swear to God, Stacey has never done this before! She would never dream of betraying me like this.'

He sent her a withering glance as he reached with one hand for his mobile, somehow managing to keep Emily secure in his arms. 'Your sister is just as untrustworthy as you. How dare you expose my daughter to such depravity?'

Tears spilled from her eyes. 'She promised me she would get help! She gave me her word.'

His dark eyes narrowed. 'To get help for what?'

Charlotte felt her chest cave in as she realised what she had revealed.

'To get help for what?' he repeated, his voice scraping along her nerves like the blade of a serrated knife.

She lowered her gaze, her stomach churning in anguish and dread, her voice coming out flat and empty. 'She's a heroin addict…ever since our mother got sick, she became involved with an unsavoury crowd… I couldn't stop her…it went downhill from there…'

'So she sells herself to feed her habit?' he asked, his dark eyes almost closed in fury.

Charlotte couldn't meet his narrowed glittering gaze. Shame felt like a searing brand all over her. She felt its imprint on every surface of her body—even her eyes were stinging with it.

She heard his harshly indrawn breath in the aching silence. 'You have allowed *my* daughter to be exposed to this?'

'I didn't have any choice,' she said, dragging her eyes back to his. 'What could I do? Abandon my sister? I am all she has. I wanted Emily to grow up knowing her aunt. I had to do what I could to keep Stacey alive, even if it meant at times compromising myself in the process.'

'You have not just compromised yourself but my daughter!'

'I had no choice!' Charlotte fought back. 'Do you know what it's like to watch someone you love destroy their potential and be unable to do anything to stop it? I have tried everything. I have begged, I have bribed, I have given her chance after chance, and time and time again, just when I think she is turning the corner, she lets me down.'

'Then get rid of her out of your life.'

She sent him an accusing look. 'Like you did to me?'

'As far as I was concerned, you were guilty. I saw no reason to continue our association.'

'It's so easy for you, isn't it? Anyone who steps over your boundaries, you cut out of your life, but she is my sister. My only living relative, apart from Emily, and I won't write her off like you did to me. She is guilty of being weak—yes— but she needs help and I will not give up on her.'

'I will not allow my daughter to be exposed to such a person,' he said as a cab pulled into the kerb. 'You will not be returning with Emily to your flat. I will make arrangements for your things to be moved to my hotel immediately.'

'A hotel is not the place for a small child,' Charlotte argued as he bundled her into the cab.

'Neither is a back yard brothel,' he threw back as he settled Emily between them.

'I told you—she's never done that before. She promised me she was going to go to detox. I planned to take her to a new clinic. That's why I took your money—to pay for it. It's expensive…I couldn't do it without—'

His eyes cut to hers. 'You used *my* money for that whore?'

Charlotte tightened her mouth. 'You sit so high up in your ivory tower seat of judgement, but what price would you have paid for your sister to get well again?'

Damon looked at her in dumbstruck silence. She was right. He would have paid any price to get Eleni well again, but no amount of money had been able to achieve it.

'You don't know what the real world is like, Damon,' she went on as the cab tyres swished over the rain-slicked roads. 'I've done everything possible to help my sister. She's broken my heart so many times but I won't give up on her. I don't believe in giving up on people, unlike you, who with just one whiff of suspicion threw our relationship away. You didn't give me a fair trial; you had made your mind up and nothing I said was ever going to change it. As far as you were concerned, I was guilty, but only because you wanted me to be guilty.'

'I did not want you to be guilty.' Damon spoke the words but he wondered deep inside if they were true. Had he been looking for a way out of their rapidly escalating relationship? His family had always married within the Greek community. A bride had already been selected for him—Iona Patonis, a pretty young woman who had all the makings of a submissive wife. She had been a close friend of Eleni's and so everyone had assumed that in time he would settle down and make her an offer...and yet...

'I did not want you to be guilty.' He repeated the words, but even the second time around they didn't ring with any more conviction.

'Yeah, right,' she said, flicking him a disdainful glance as she drew her daughter closer. 'Your so-called love for me didn't last the distance, did it, Damon? If you had truly cared anything for me, nothing would have stopped you from defending me, but you let me go the first chance you could.'

'If it is any comfort to you, it was not easy for me to do so,' he said, looking down at his hands resting on his tiny daughter's pink pyjama-clad bent knees.

She gave him an embittered look and turned her head to look at the raindrops beading on the window of the cab. 'Then you escaped lightly,' she said. 'The hardest thing for me was walking away from you and staying away.'

But she hadn't walked away of her own free will, Damon reminded himself with a deep pang of regret as he settled back in his seat, his hands still on his tiny daughter's legs.

He had sent her away...

CHAPTER TEN

EMILY started to stir in Charlotte's arms once they arrived at Damon's hotel.

'Where are we, Mummy?' she asked, blinking at the bright lights of the hotel foyer as the cab drew to a halt outside.

'We're at a hotel, darling,' Charlotte answered. 'This is where your…er…daddy is staying.'

'My daddy is here?' Emily asked with wide eyes.

Charlotte caught the tail-end of Damon's look and felt another wave of guilt crash through her. He was so very angry but in amongst the anger she could see he was deeply hurt. His dark eyes shone with it, the pain evident every time he looked at his little daughter.

'Yes, he's here, darling.'

'Emily—' Damon's deep voice brought the little girl's head around '—I am your daddy.'

'Weally?' Emily's eyes grew even wider.

He smiled and gently stroked a long finger against her creamy cheek. 'Yes I am—really.'

'Are you going to live wif us now?' Emily asked, her thumb sneaking up to her little mouth.

'That hasn't been de—' Charlotte began.

'That is certainly what I will be doing,' Damon said, interrupting her. 'In fact we are going to go on a holiday together, just like a real family.'

'In an aeropwane?' Emily asked around her thumb.

He nodded as he lifted her out of the cab. 'Not just any old aeroplane, little one, but my very own private jet.'

'I've never been on an aeropwane,' Emily said, nestling against his shoulder, her eyelids beginning to droop once more. 'Is Mummy coming too?'

Damon met Charlotte's mutinous look. 'Yes, she is, Emily.'

'Are you going to get married?' Emily asked.

Charlotte's eyes moved away from the burning probe of Damon's to address her daughter. 'Not all mummies and daddies are married to each other,' she explained.

Emily's little forehead started to wrinkle. 'But I want to be a flower girl like Janie was. I want to wear a pretty dress and have flowers and stuff in my hair.'

'I will see what can be arranged,' Damon said and led the way into the hotel.

Charlotte had to wait until Emily was settled and sound asleep in the second bedroom of the penthouse suite before she could confront Damon over his autocratic plans to take over their lives.

'How dare you imply to Emily we're getting married?' she fumed as she came into the main room. 'She'll be so disappointed when she finds out the truth.'

He held her flashing blue gaze for a lengthy moment without speaking. Charlotte didn't care for the intransigent set to his features and wondered what was going on behind the dark screen of his eyes. She could almost hear the cogs of his incisive mind ticking over.

'Emily has raised an important issue,' he said at last. 'She is a child crying out for a normal family life. We can give that to her.'

Charlotte stared at him in alarm. 'Don't even think about it, Damon. You're the last man I would ever consider marrying.'

'I am not going to give you a choice,' he said with an intractable set to his mouth. 'If you do not agree to become my wife, you will find yourself not only without a job but without a daughter. There is not a judge in Australia who would allow a little child of three years of age to be exposed to a heroin-addicted prostitute, and you damn well know it.'

'I am her mother! You can't just waltz in and take her away.'

He moved past her to get himself a drink from the well-stocked bar on the other side of the room. 'Well, I am her father and, since I have not had any say in her upbringing thus far, I am taking full control now.'

Charlotte drew in a breath that scraped at her raw throat. 'How can you expect to know what's in her best interests? You don't even know how to be a father.'

His eyes hit hers. 'And whose fault is that?'

She couldn't hold the burning accusation in his gaze. 'I told you I had no choice. I would have told you years ago, but you wouldn't listen.'

He moved back to stand in front of her, his height so intimidating she felt herself shrink backwards. 'Tell me something, Charlotte—' his voice was like an ice floe passing over her skin '—were you ever going to get around to telling me of her existence? You have known I was coming to Sydney for months. You could have at any time contacted me and told me and yet you did not. Not only that, over the last few days you have spent hours and hours in my company and yet you have not said a word.'

Charlotte felt the probe of his gaze against hers and knew it would be pointless to lie to him now. 'I was trying to work up the courage...' she said, her throat moving up and down painfully.

'I do not believe you.'

'I was!'

'You are lying. You have had numerous opportunities to tell me. No wonder you found it hard to look at me. All that talk of you finding things difficult between us was a pack of lies. What you were finding difficult was facing up to your guilt.'

'I was going to tell you! I wanted to, but I was worried you'd do exactly what you're doing now!'

'You bitch.' His embittered words slashed the air like a machete. 'You thieving little lying bitch.'

Charlotte raised her hand without thinking but he caught it in mid-air, his rapid block sending every bit of air out of her lungs.

'You want to play it rough, do you, Charlotte?' he asked, his fingers tightening around her wrist until she was sure it would bruise. 'Go on, then. Hit me.'

Her eyes blazed with hatred. 'Let go of me or you'll regret it.'

He gave a mocking laugh as she pulled ineffectually against his hold. 'How are you going to make me regret it, *agape mou*?'

She kicked out with her foot but he spun her around so her back was towards him, every hard ridge and plane of his body now pressing against hers. She could feel his warmth seeping into her, the fragrance of his aftershave filling her senses and the unmistakable swelling of his erection probing her erotically from behind.

'I do not think violence becomes you, Charlotte,' he said against her neck, his lips a temptation she knew she would not be able to bear for much longer. 'I prefer you purring like a kitten in my arms.'

'L-let me go…' Her plea was halfway between a gasp and a groan as he pressed even harder against her.

His mouth found the sensitive skin behind her ear. 'That

was my mistake four years ago,' he said. 'This time I will not let you go.'

She shivered as his tongue slid from behind her ear to her neck, tasting her in tiny teasing kisses that made her stomach quiver and her legs go weak and watery.

He turned her in his arms and looked down at her, his eyes alight with desire as his hand cupped her breast, his other reaching between her legs, rubbing her intimately until she was leaning into him unashamedly. 'See how you respond to me, Charlotte?'

'I don't want to respond to you…' she breathed into the hot moist cavern of his mouth as it hovered just above hers. 'It doesn't seem right…'

His lips brushed against hers, the tickling, teasing touch stirring her into a mindless frenzy of need. 'What would indeed be wrong would be to ignore this passion that sizzles between us, Charlotte,' he said, stroking her bottom lip with the rasping, sensuous glide of his tongue.

She opened her mouth as his tongue pushed tantalisingly against her lips, her stomach hollowing in need as he thrust in once, stroked her tongue with his and then retreated. She brought her mouth back to his and met his tongue with her own, tentatively at first and then, when he responded with a deep groan, with even more fervour.

It was a kiss of combat and the angst fuelling it somehow made it all the more thrilling. Her teeth nipped at him, inciting him to do the same, her bottom lip his tender target. He suckled on its fullness before capturing it with his teeth again in a series of playful little bites that had her senses instantly screaming for release.

He pushed her backwards until she was up against the nearest wall, his mouth feeding hungrily off hers, his chest heaving in and out with the effort of staying in control.

Charlotte didn't want him in control. She wanted him in full-throttle mode, no holds barred. She tore at his shirt with her fingers, searching for the springy hair on his chest, her nails raking along his skin with an almost animal passion as her tongue fought with his for supremacy.

His hands went to her breasts, shaping her through the fabric of her dress possessively before he reached behind her for her zip and lowered it. The feel of his hands on the naked skin of her back was intoxicating, every pore of her skin tensing in delight as he brought his hands around to where her breasts were aching for his touch.

Her dress fell in a pool at her feet, leaving her with nothing but her knickers and thigh-high stockings and heels, her whole body quivering in anticipation as he reached beneath the damp lace of her underwear to stroke her intimately.

'You want me,' he said in a husky tone, his dark eyes glittering with victory. 'You can deny it all you like, but your body speaks for you.'

Charlotte couldn't see any point in denying it now. Her whole body arched to bring his fingers deeper but it still wasn't enough. She threw her head back and gave a whimpering groan as his fingers began to massage the wet swollen bud of her femininity with devastating expertise. She could feel the tension building all through her body until her mind switched off and she became conscious of nothing but the spiralling sensations his masterful touch was evoking. She felt the first flicker and then the full-on rush of feeling as the spasms took hold, rocking her body against his hand, her hips undulating with the sheer force of trying to hold on to that exquisite feeling for as long as she could.

Her whole body sagged against the wall when it was over, her legs feeling as if they were going to fold beneath her.

Shame coursed through her like a hot red tide when Damon stepped back from her. Whatever desire he had felt was now gone. She could see the disdain in his eyes as they raked her slumped form and she inwardly cringed at her appalling lack of control.

She rustled up a tattered remnant of pride and, affecting a sultry expression, met his gaze. 'What's wrong, Damon? Not feeling up to it again tonight? I thought you had more stamina.'

His mouth tightened. 'I do not intend to sleep with you again until we are married.'

Her eyes flashed back at him defiantly. 'I don't intend to sleep with you at all, married or not!'

His lip curled as his gaze ran over her half-naked form. 'I can have you whenever I like. I just proved it.'

'You proved nothing but what an unscrupulous man you are,' she spat back.

He stepped towards her again, his arms locking hers above her head. 'You like to brandish those insults of yours around, don't you? But I should warn you that once we are married you will have to tame that tongue of yours or you will regret it.'

'How are you going to make me regret it, Damon?' She threw his own words back at him, her taunting tone setting off a blazing inferno in his eyes as they clashed with hers.

She sucked in a little breath as his hands pulled her from where she was pressed up against the wall, her body slamming into the tempting heat of his.

'I will teach you to bend to my will if it's the last thing I do,' he growled.

'Then you're going to have one hell of a fight on your hands,' she warned him with a lift of her chin.

His eyes warred with hers, his jaw so tight she could hear his teeth grinding together.

The tension was like an electric current zinging in the air. The scent of his arousal was there too, teasing her nostrils until she felt as if she was breathing him into the secret depths of her body.

His eyes burned into hers as he pulled her towards the huge bed, his free hand undoing his belt, his shoes thudding to the floor as he pressed her down on the mattress, his weight pinning her beneath him.

'Is this what you want?' he asked, releasing himself, the hard probe of his erect body already sinking into her wet warmth.

Charlotte gasped as he drove forward with a deep thick thrust, her inner muscles grabbing at him greedily, wanting all of him, again and again. Her hands clawed at him, holding him, caressing him, stroking him until he let out a deep primal groan as he sank even further into her warmth, his movements quickening as the pressure built.

His pace was almost too hard and too fast but somehow she kept up, her body responding without restraint, her soft but frantic cries making her pant as she felt herself climbing to the summit again.

Damon lifted his mouth off hers and forced her chin up so that she met his eyes. 'Look at me,' he demanded hoarsely.

Her eyes skirted away from his but he wouldn't allow it. 'Look at me, damn you! I want you to see what you do to me, what you have always done to me.'

'You hate yourself for it, though, don't you, Damon?' she asked a little breathlessly as his hard body thrust deeply and de-terminedly into hers. 'You want me even though you hate me.'

'The less said about my feelings towards you right now the better,' he said, and with one last powerful thrust he triggered her release with the mind-blowing explosion of his own.

Charlotte lay in the tight circle of his arms, her heart still racing as the aftershocks of pleasure filtered through her body. She could feel the deep thud of his heart against her breast and his uneven breathing against the soft skin of her neck. She wanted to say something but for the life of her couldn't think of how to break the awkward silence. She felt so ashamed of her weakness; she had practically begged him to make love to her again.

She felt him roll away and turned her head to see him put his hand up over his eyes as if warding off a nasty headache. She watched as his chest rose and fell in a sigh before he removed his hand and turned his head to look at her.

'I am sorry, Charlotte,' he said in a gruff tone. 'That was not meant to happen, or at least not like that.'

She gave him an ironic look. 'I thought that was why you paid me in the first place. Wasn't that the deal? I was to become your paid mistress for the period of time you're here?'

A dull flush appeared along his sharp cheekbones. 'I did not know then that you were the mother of my child,' he said.

She raised her brows expressively. 'So that makes it somehow different, does it?'

'You know it does.'

She got off the bed and scooped her clothing off the floor, dressing again with angry, agitated movements. She pulled the hair out of the back of her dress once she had zipped it back up and glared at him.

'You're a hypocrite, Damon. You were content to employ me as your mistress when it suited you but now you want me to be a faithful, obedient wife.'

He got off the bed and reached for a robe. 'You will be my wife, Charlotte,' he said, tying the ends together almost viciously. 'But, as to whether you will be faithful and obedient, that remains to be seen.'

'How will you explain this to your mother?' she asked. 'I can imagine she's going to be rather shocked that you lowered yourself to marry the hired help.'

'She will understand my motivation to protect my daughter at whatever cost.'

'But what about the cost to me?' she asked. 'You're asking me to walk away from my life here.'

'As far as I can see it, your life here consists of juggling a career and a child and the consequences of the criminal behaviour of your sister. You will be much better out of it. As my wife you will have everything money can buy. Emily will not only have the benefit of two parents, but she will also have the devotion of her grandmother.'

'You think by waving your wallet around you can have anything you like, don't you?'

His eyes glittered as they clashed with hers. 'I bought you, did I not?'

She drew in a sharp little breath, her blue eyes flashing with spite. 'Then I hope you enjoyed this evening, for it's not going to happen again.'

'It will happen again, Charlotte, for you cannot help yourself. We are alike in that, if nothing else. We still share the fierce attraction we felt from the first moment we met.'

'But we hate each other,' she said. 'What sort of home environment are we going to provide for Emily? We'll be bickering and sniping at each other all the time.'

'We will act like the responsible, mature adults we are meant to be,' he countered. 'We will treat each other with respect, most especially when in the company of our daughter.'

'That's going to be quite a challenge for you then, isn't it?' She gave him a pointed look. 'I can see nothing but hatred in your eyes.'

'You should consider yourself fortunate that I am actually prepared to marry you. On the basis of what I witnessed this evening, I could take Emily off you permanently.'

'So I'm supposed to be grateful that you're forcing me into marriage, am I?'

'You could do a lot worse.'

'Yes, I suppose I could,' she shot back sarcastically. 'I could have married someone who loved me.'

'You had the chance to do that four years ago but you threw it away.'

'There is no way of convincing you, is there?' she asked, ashamed that tears were prickling at the backs of her eyes. 'You still see me as a thief. You will always see me as that.'

'I am prepared to put aside the past to deal with our future,' he said. 'We have a child to consider now. It would not be good for Emily to hear about that incident. I will make sure no one speaks of it ever again. Besides, as far as I know, only my mother, Eleni and I knew about it.'

Charlotte frowned. 'You didn't tell anyone else?'

'No.'

'But…but why not?'

'I thought it best at the time.'

'But how did you explain our sudden parting?' she asked. 'Surely people wanted to know what had happened between us.'

'I told them you had study commitments back home, which was partly true. You would have had to return at some point to finish your degree, even if I had asked you to marry me. I would not have expected you to sacrifice your education.'

'And yet you are demanding I sacrifice the whole point of my education now—my career.'

'You have a child, Charlotte. You have clearly struggled to provide for her alone. Once we are married and settled into a routine you can think about returning to your career. There are numerous opportunities on Santorini for a person with your qualifications.'

'You really expect me to do this, don't you? To just walk away from my life and take up with you.'

'You do not have any choice. It is either marry me or lose your daughter.'

'Even though by doing so I will be losing myself?'

'You will not lose yourself, Charlotte,' he said. 'I will try to be a good husband to you.'

'Does that mean you'll be faithful?'

He held her challenging look for a long time before answering. 'That remains entirely up to you.'

She narrowed her eyes at him. 'What do you mean by that?'

'If you do not want to conduct a normal physical relationship with me, then I will have no choice but to have my needs met elsewhere.'

She gave him a disgusted glance. 'You mean pay someone?'

His eyes swept over her in a raking manner. 'Up until now I have never had to pay.'

She tightened her mouth. 'I only took that money to help my sister. I was never going to sleep with you.'

'So what changed your mind?'

Charlotte turned away in case he saw her vulnerability. She could hardly tell him she was still in love with him, even though it was painfully true.

'I asked what changed your mind,' he said again.

She turned back around once she was sure her expression was bland with indifference. 'Sex with an ex holds some sort of appeal, don't you think? I wanted to see if you still had what it took.'

'And your verdict is?'

She had to look away. 'Revisiting relationships is always fraught with the danger of disappointment.'

'If you were disappointed you showed no sign of it,' he commented wryly.

'A hungry person would think contaminated food is a feast,' she returned with an arch look.

'So you thought it was worth the risk?'

She gave a little shrug.

'But we do it rather well, don't we, Charlotte?'

She gritted her teeth and crossed her arms over her chest, scowling furiously. 'I hate myself for responding to you.'

He moved across to stand in front of her, his hand tipping up her face so she had to look at him. 'You are always going to respond to me, *agape mou*,' he said. 'It is something that is inescapable.'

Charlotte could feel the magnetic pull of his gaze as it held hers, all her senses going into overload as his eyes dipped to her mouth. Her lips buzzed in anticipation of the erotic pressure of his mouth on hers, her skin prickling all over at the thought of his body invading hers so commandingly, her eyelids slowly closing as she prepared herself for his devastating kiss…

'Mummy?'

Charlotte's eyes sprang open as Emily padded into the room.

'Darling…' She rushed across the room to crouch down before her daughter. 'Is your arm hurting?'

'Yes…' Emily gave a little sob. 'And I had another bad dweam.'

'I'm here now, sweetie,' she soothed.

'And so am I,' Damon said.

Emily rubbed at her eyes and padded over to him. 'I was dweaming about you,' she said, looking up at him with huge black eyes.

'W-were you?' Damon felt his throat tighten as he looked down at the little pixie face in front of him.

'I fought you were going to go away…'

He bent down to her level, his eyes warm as they met hers. 'I am not going away, little one. You can count on that.'

'I can't count past ten,' Emily said with a sheepish look. 'Mummy's been teaching me but I'm not berry good.'

Damon felt as if someone had clamped his heart in a vice.

He had never felt such emotion before. 'You are only three years old,' he reminded her. 'You have plenty of time to learn.'

'Can you count to a hundred?' Emily asked, slipping her thumb into her mouth and sucking so hard he could hear it.

He smiled as another emotional gear shifted in his chest. 'Yes, I can.'

The tiny thumb came out long enough to ask, 'Will you teach me?'

He gathered her into his arms and breathed in the small child scent of her, his heart contracting at the thought of all he had missed out on so far.

'I will teach you whatever you need to learn, little one.'

'Mummy?' Emily peered past her father's broad shoulder. 'Did you hear dat? Daddy's going to teach me to count to a hundred.'

Charlotte smiled even though her face hurt with the effort. 'That's wonderful, darling. I'm sure he'll be a wonderful teacher.'

Emily snuggled up close to her father as he carried her back to the spare bedroom. 'I like having a daddy,' she said, hugging him tight around the neck with her little arms.

'And I like having a daughter,' Damon said, trying to control his voice.

Emily eased herself away to look at him with big serious black-brown eyes. 'You won't go away again, will you?' she asked. ''Cause I haven't shown you my special fings.'

'What special things do you want to show me?' he asked as he tucked her back into the spare bed.

She gave him an assessing look, as if deciding whether he was to be trusted or not. 'I have a teddy bear and a doll and a wabbit with one ear.'

'What happened to the other ear?' he asked, trying his best to disguise the choked emotion in his voice.

'I cut it off when I was berry little,' she confessed. 'I found Mummy's scissors and cut it off. I got into big twouble, didn't I, Mummy?'

Charlotte's throat felt too tight to get the words out. 'Yes…I was very worried you could have hurt yourself.'

'Will you read me a story?' Emily asked her father. 'Mummy always reads me a story and sometimes if I'm berry good she makes one up in her head. Can you do dat?'

'I'll give it a try,' Damon said. 'What sort of stories do you like?'

Emily wriggled underneath the covers. 'I like the ones with a happy ending. Do you have any of those in your head?'

'I guess I could try to find one,' he said, scratching his temple.

'The best ones start with once upon a time,' she told him with solemn authority. 'I can start you off if you like.'

He smiled down at her, his heart feeling so big it felt as if it was taking over his body. 'That would be great.'

She took a little preparatory breath that reminded him so much of Charlotte he could scarcely inflate his own lungs.

'Once upon a time…' She gave him an impish grin. 'Now it's your turn.'

'O-K,' he said and settled himself on the bed beside her. 'Once upon a time there was a beautiful little girl who was called Emily…'

CHAPTER ELEVEN

'Is SHE asleep?' Charlotte asked when Damon joined her in the main suite some time later.

'Yes.' He pushed his hand through his hair and began to pace the room, anger and tension visible in each and every stride.

She twisted her hands together, her mouth drying in anguish. 'Damon...'

He turned to glare at her. 'I have missed out on so much. Do you have any idea what that feels like? I have nothing! No memories of her as a baby—nothing. You have taken that from me.'

'I tried to tell you.'

'You should have kept trying.'

'For how long?' she asked, her tone bordering on despair. 'My mother was dying, my sister was going off the rails and I was juggling my studies with a difficult pregnancy. I know it's hard for you to understand, but I felt I had no choice but to leave you to your life while I did my best to get on with mine. The words you said to me that last day...' She stumbled over the memory and continued, her voice ragged with emotion. 'I was so hurt. The way you spoke made me worried that if by some chance you did come around to believe me you might force me into having a termination. I couldn't take the risk. That's why I didn't try and contact you again until I had passed the point of no return.'

'I would not have asked that of you.' His voice sounded as if it was coming from very deep inside him.

She gave him an embittered look. 'Wouldn't you? Come on, Damon, don't you remember what you said to me? You told me I wasn't to be believed, that I was a slut who had her eye on snaring herself a billionaire. Not exactly the words I wanted to hear when I was trying to do the right thing by telling you.'

He let out a heavy sigh. 'I deeply regret how I handled the situation. But if you had persisted in trying to contact me I would have come around eventually.'

'Yes and whipped her away from me as you're threatening to do now.'

'I want her in my life. I am not leaving without her. You have the choice of marrying me and coming with us or letting her go.'

'That's not what I call a choice. It's blackmail.'

'I do not care what you call it, Charlotte. I want my daughter and I am prepared to marry you to have her.'

'Well, thanks very much for the romantic proposal,' she said with a cutting edge to her voice.

'What do you expect me to say?' He glowered at her. 'I am still so angry with you I can barely think straight.'

'You should be angry at yourself, not me. If you hadn't been so arrogantly assured of my guilt you wouldn't have missed out on Emily at all. Have you considered that, Damon? What if I wasn't guilty? What then?'

His throat moved up and down convulsively and it was a moment or two before he answered. 'You have to be guilty.'

'Why?' She looked at him coldly. 'So you can still be the good guy, the injured one, the one with victim written all over your face?'

'There have been no thefts since,' he said. 'And certainly none before you came.'

'So that somehow makes me automatically responsible?' She looked at him incredulously. 'Oh, for God's sake, Damon, surely you're not that blindsided?'

'I do not wish to talk about that incident.' He turned away from her and began to pace again. 'I wish to discuss how we will manage things from now on.'

'I can't leave until the exhibition is launched,' she said. 'I can't let Julian down like that.'

'All right.' He turned to face her once more. 'We will stay for you to complete your commitments to the exhibition, but in the meantime we will formalise our relationship. I will see to it tomorrow.'

'It takes a month to procure a marriage licence,' she pointed out.

'I can apply for a special licence.'

'Emily doesn't have a passport.'

He frowned at her. 'Why the hell not?'

She rolled her eyes scathingly. 'Strange as it may seem to someone with the disgusting wealth you have taken for granted all of your life, other people, especially single mothers, do not have the money to travel the length and breadth of the globe. I have had to put food on the table and pay for childcare so I could work, even though I didn't want to when Emily was a baby. It broke my heart leaving her with strangers while my breasts ached and leaked all day.'

His features twisted with anguish. 'You struggled like that without once trying again to contact me?'

She turned away in disgust. 'What would have been the point? I was sick of beating my head against a brick wall. Look at the way you treated me the first day you were here. You've made it pretty clear how low your opinion of me was.'

A tense little silence tightened the air.

'I admit I left you with little choice that first night, but why did you agree to see me again?' he asked. 'You could have told me you were not interested and left it at that.'

'I did tell you I wasn't interested but you kept dangling threats over my head,' she reminded him coldly. 'Then when you said you wanted us to meet as friends... I thought it would be good for us to establish a relationship based on mutual respect... I thought that it would be a better way of revealing the truth about Emily. I didn't want to spring it on you; neither did I want you to find out some other way.'

His hand carved another rough pathway through his hair. 'I want to believe you, Charlotte, but everything in me warns me against lowering my guard. You ripped my heart from my chest four years ago and you have done it again by keeping my daughter from me. How can I trust you?'

Tears burned in her eyes. 'More to the point, how can I trust you?' she asked. 'You have threatened me from the word go, blackmailing me into a relationship and leaving me no choice but to lie to protect Emily and myself. I hated lying to you. I loathe all forms of deceit. I grew up with my father's lies and I have enough on my plate with my sister's without making up my own.'

'Charlotte...'

He took a step towards her but she held up her hand to ward him off. 'No, don't. Please. I can't bear it. I hate what's happened to us. We had such a lovely relationship... You were the most wonderful man I'd ever met...so warm and vibrant. I loved you with all of my heart. I would never have done anything to hurt you, but you've destroyed it all. You're angry at missing out on Emily's life so far, but what about what I've missed out on?' Tears were running down her cheeks and she brushed at them angrily. 'Have you ever stopped to think of that? *Have you?*'

Damon swallowed back the raw pain in his throat. He wasn't used to so much emotion overloading his system. Four years ago he had shut off his feelings; only the loss of Eleni had resurrected them before he had locked them away again behind a bolted door in his brain. But he felt now as if Charlotte was picking the lock, her own emotions seeping under the door to reach his…

'What have you missed out on, Charlotte?' he asked hollowly. 'Tell me.'

He saw her chest lift and fall in a ragged sigh. 'I felt so alone when I came back to Australia… My mother was diagnosed with breast cancer the same week I had the pregnancy confirmed. I was so torn. There were so many people depending on me. Stacey was devastated by Mum's diagnosis and began to experiment with drugs to blunt the pain. She never really got over my father's suicide while he was in prison. She adored him and, being so young, she didn't quite understand why he would do that. I threw myself into my studies, knowing I would have to provide for my child and possibly Stacey as well. I had no one to turn to, no one to tell how scared I was. I hadn't even held a baby before and suddenly I was expecting one.'

Damon felt his chest tighten to the point of pain. How had he been so blind and unfeeling? Even if she was as guilty as he believed her to be, it did not excuse his treatment of her since. 'I do not know what to say…'

She gave him a bleak look. 'I guess sorry is out of the question. You're too proud to admit you got it wrong.'

'I am sorry you have had to deal with this alone. But you will no longer have to do so. We will be together from now on to give Emily all that she deserves as a much loved daughter.'

'But she won't have two parents who love each other,' she reminded him. 'That's what every child deserves.'

'In this day and age it is rare for both parents to remain together, let alone maintain that level of affection. We will no doubt become friends over time.'

'We didn't do so well on the friends thing before,' she reminded him.

'Yes, well, I am perhaps to blame for that,' he admitted. 'I cannot seem to help myself around you. I am still fiercely attracted to you.'

'Which you hate yourself for, remember?'

'You have said much the same, Charlotte.'

She shifted her gaze. 'So you're expecting our marriage to be normal…as in sex and all that.'

'I am a little intrigued as to what exactly you are referring to as "all that" but yes—I would hope that we will maintain as normal a relationship as possible. It will be good for Emily to grow up in a family atmosphere.'

Charlotte looked down at her hands for a moment. 'She likes you…Emily, I mean… In fact, I think she already loves you…'

He cleared his throat. 'She is a beautiful child. I cannot believe she is really mine.'

Her eyes sprang back to his defensively. 'If you feel the need to have a paternity test done I won't stop you.'

He frowned at her expression. 'I was not for the moment suggesting—'

'Yes, you were, go on—admit it. I can see the flicker of doubt in your eyes. *What if she's lying again, foisting some other man's brat on me to get more money?* That's what you're thinking, isn't it?'

He let out a frustrated breath. 'This is a going nowhere discussion. I can see Emily is mine. I do not need a test to confirm it.'

'What if she didn't look like you?' she asked with an accusing glare. 'I bet you'd be swabbing her mouth with a dip stick and rushing it off to the nearest DNA laboratory as soon as you could.'

'Is there some doubt in your own mind as to who is her father?' he asked.

Her eyes turned to twin points of angry blue flame. *'How can you ask that?'* she choked.

'It is a reasonable question, I would have thought. It's been four years; surely there have been other men in your life.'

'There hasn't been anyone since you.'

He raised his brows cynically. 'For someone who claims to abhor being deceitful, you show a remarkable talent for it.'

Charlotte swung away in fury. 'Here we go again. You refuse to believe a single word I say. This is never going to work.'

'It will work because we will make it work,' he said. 'We are both committed to Emily. She is my biggest priority now. I want to spend time getting to know her, catching up on all I missed out on before.'

She held her arms close to her body without turning around. 'I have photos and film footage of her first steps and words. I've kept everything...even all of her baby clothes...'

'I would like to see them some time.'

'I'll collect them from my flat.'

'About your flat...' Damon paused before continuing. 'Does your sister live there with you permanently?'

Charlotte turned back to look at him. 'No...she comes and goes a bit but I've never encouraged her to move in with us.'

His expression was thoughtful as he watched her for a moment.

'I think she's beyond help,' she added in a defeated tone, her eyes falling away from his. 'I've done everything I can...I only agreed to your terms so I could help her but she used that money to pay back her dealer.' Her shoulders dropped another level as she continued. 'I would have even slept with you that first night if it would have brought her back. I would have done anything, but sometimes anything and everything is just not enough…'

'You look exhausted.' Somehow Damon got his voice into gear. 'You can have the bed. I'll sleep on the sofa.'

'Are you sure?'

Her grateful look was like an arrow to his heart. He stretched his mouth into the semblance of a smile. 'Go to bed, Charlotte. You have no need to fear my attentions tonight.' He moved towards the door.

'Damon?'

He brought his gaze back to hers. 'I am going out for a short while. I would like to spend the next few days with Emily, if I may. You will have a full three weeks ahead with the launch of the exhibition. Emily and I can spend the time getting to know one another. With her arm so tender I would not like to have her bumped by other children at childcare.'

Fresh tears washed into Charlotte's eyes at his concern for his little daughter, but before she could assemble the words to tell him how touched she was he had already left.

CHAPTER TWELVE

'YOU should see the hordes of people coming in,' Diane said three weeks later. 'This is going down as one of the highlights of the museum's year.'

Charlotte wondered what her colleague would say if she told her it had been one of the worst periods of her life. She had gone from highs to lows within the space of seconds each day as she had juggled work and her tricky relationship with Damon. Her only consolation had been Emily's rapid acceptance of her father. Her little face had beamed from ear to ear each day as he had taken her out to entertain her. Charlotte had had to bite her tongue to stop herself from commenting on the expensive toys he had bought, for she realised he was doing his best to make up for lost time.

Stacey had left a message on her mobile saying she was finally getting help but Charlotte found it hard to feel confident that she would in fact do so. She had heard nothing from her since, even though she had left countless messages on her answering service.

The flat had been cleaned out and Charlotte's and Emily's things transferred to the hotel but she still didn't feel as if she belonged there.

Damon was polite to her but he seemed intent on avoiding

her at every opportunity. He would insist on putting Emily to bed each night but he would go out afterwards and it would be the early hours of the morning before Charlotte would hear him return to his makeshift bed on the sofa. She had put her pride aside one night and suggested he share the bed with her, but he had declined the offer with what she could only describe as cold disdain.

'You must be excited about your wedding this weekend,' Diane said. 'Everyone's talking about it.'

'It's to be a very quiet affair.'

'It's so romantic—Damon Latousakis being Emily's father and all. Mind you, I knew it from the moment I saw him.'

Charlotte gave her a weak smile without responding.

'This trip to Greece is just what you need,' Diane continued. 'You look like you need a holiday. This has been a huge workload for you, but Julian is well on the mend and champing at the bit to get back. By the time you return he'll be back on board.'

'I'm only going to be away for two weeks.'

'You should be taking longer; after all, this is your honeymoon. You won't even have to work any more if you don't want to. Why not lie back and enjoy it?'

Why not, indeed? Charlotte thought. The only trouble was her husband couldn't bear to be in the same room as her.

For some reason Charlotte couldn't quite fathom, Damon had insisted on a church wedding. The ceremony, though brief, was traditional and Emily proudly attended them as a flower girl, her little floral basket adorned with ribbons swinging from her hands as she walked up the aisle with a solemn look on her tiny face.

Damon winked at her and her little face instantly split into a broad smile and Charlotte felt her heart begin to crack. He had done so much in such a short time to build a bridge with his daughter. They had the sort of relationship she had never had with her own father—loving, playful and totally accepting.

The only slight hitch in the proceedings was the kiss during the ceremony. Charlotte told herself it was more or less a formal procedure that the congregation expected, but it didn't stop her lips from clinging to Damon's with escalating need.

He was the first to move away, which hurt her, but she disguised it behind a forced smile as they moved to sign the register.

Emily was bouncing up and down with excitement as the reception drew to a close. 'Are we going on the aeropwane yet?'

'Soon, darling,' Charlotte said as she gathered her close to her side. 'One more sleep.'

'I'm going to meet my granny, aren't I? Daddy told me.'

'Yes, you are, precious.'

'Can I take all of my toys to show her?'

'Only your very special ones,' she said.

'She can take whatever she wants,' Damon said, putting his hand on Emily's silky head in a proprietary manner.

Charlotte's blue gaze tussled with his coal-black one before she finally gave in. 'I'm sure Daddy will help you pack everything you need.'

'Are you mad at Daddy?' Emily asked as her thumb slid towards her mouth.

'No, of course not,' she lied, shooting Damon a blistering glare over the top of Emily's head.

'I don't want you to be mad at Daddy. I love him.'

Charlotte felt her throat tighten and bent down to her daughter's level. 'I know you do, darling, and I...I...I er...love him too. I've just had a lot to deal with lately with the wedding and the exhibition and all.'

'Do you weally love him?' Emily looked at her entreatingly.

Charlotte pasted a bright smile on her face. 'How could I not love the father of my little girl?'

Damon took his daughter's hand. 'Come on, little one. We have to say goodbye to some guests.'

Charlotte let out her breath once they had gone and turned to face another guest who wanted to congratulate her. She comforted herself with the thought that Damon thought her a consummate liar. How would he know she was this time actually telling the truth?

Once Emily had settled for the night Damon came out to the main suite where Charlotte was flicking idly through a magazine. She was aware of him standing there watching her but kept her head down, pretending an absorption in an article on home improvement hints.

'I would like to speak to you,' he said.

She turned over to another page without looking up. 'What about?'

He closed the distance between them and removed the magazine from her hands.

'Hey, I was reading that!' She scowled at him.

He tossed the magazine to the floor, his dark features etched with anger. 'You are so determined to ignore me but I will not tolerate it, Charlotte.'

'You've ignored me for the past three weeks,' she threw back resentfully. 'You've barely addressed a single word to me unless Emily's been present. Then of course you're all sweetness and charm. What a hypocrite.'

'You are just as guilty of pretending something you do not feel. Emily is going to be confused by your mixed messages if you do not control your propensity to insult me at every opportunity. She is an intelligent and highly sensitive child, who is already picking up on the antagonistic atmosphere between us. She shows signs of deep insecurity. I have noticed when you and I are together she sucks her thumb much more than when she is alone with me.'

'So what are you suggesting?' Her eyes challenged his. 'That we kiss and make up?'

'That would be a very good start.'

She sprang off the sofa in agitation. 'You can go to hell.'

He caught her by the arm and turned her around to face him. 'We are husband and wife now, Charlotte. We are travelling to Santorini tomorrow, where it will be expected we will share a bed. I do not want anyone, particularly my mother, to think there is anything amiss in our relationship.'

'You mean you haven't told her the truth?'

'No, of course not,' he said, dropping his hand from her arm. 'I wanted her to enjoy her first grandchild without worrying there may be no others for her to look forward to in the not so distant future.'

She stared at him in shock, her stomach turning over itself. 'You want another child?' She swallowed deeply. *'With me?'*

'You find the notion unsettling?'

'I find the notion outrageous!'

His jaw tensed and a hardened look came into his dark eyes. 'I do not see the problem. We already have one child. It is only natural to want to add to our family a little brother or sister for Emily to grow up with.'

'Our family, as you call it, is a sham! You're making me out to be some sort of breeding machine. How can you possibly think of bringing another child into this mess?'

'It will only be a mess if you do not agree to cooperate in an adult and mature fashion.'

'I fail to see what is adult and mature about *your* behaviour,' she said. 'You've held me to ransom from the word go.'

'I do have some regrets over the way I handled our relationship,' he confessed with a small frown disturbing his forehead. 'I should not have treated you the way I did that first night.'

'Oh, wow, is that an apology I hear?' she scoffed. 'Does "some regrets" mean you're actually admitting to having made a mistake? How on earth will you cope with having put a black mark on your pristine copybook?'

'Actually it is an apology of sorts,' he said, meeting her eyes once more. 'I had underestimated your commitment to your sister. Your devotion to her is remarkable considering what she has put you through. It shows you have a forgiving side to your nature.'

'Unlike you,' she couldn't resist throwing back at him.

'No, perhaps you are right,' he said with another regretful frown. 'I do find it hard to let go of resentment. I tend to brood on things, which has a tendency over time to blow everything out of proportion.'

Charlotte had to fight the urge to be mollified by his grudging confession. She wanted to be angry with him. She needed to be angry with him to keep herself safe from further hurt.

'I want this to work, not just for Emily, but for us,' he said into the taut silence. 'She is a beautiful little girl. I cannot tell you what it means to me to have her in my life. I do not know how to thank you for choosing to go ahead with the pregnancy. So many young women, given the circumstances, would not have done so.'

Charlotte had to clamp her bottom lip between her teeth to hold back her emotion. She had agonised over what to do in those first few weeks, especially when her mother had become so desperately ill and her sister so obviously in need of her support. But she had not been able to bring herself to rid herself of the one thing that still connected her to Damon.

'I loved her from the moment I knew I was carrying her…'

Damon stepped forward and brushed a gentle hand across

her cheek, the gesture so poignant and unexpected she had trouble keeping the moisture from spilling from her eyes as she raised them to his.

'I love her too,' he said, his voice unmistakably husky. 'I would do anything for her.'

She gave him a twisted look. 'You've certainly demonstrated that by marrying me—the woman you hate more than any other.'

He held her gaze for interminable seconds, his dark, unfathomable eyes boring into hers until she was sure he was seeing her soul laid bare.

'Perhaps in time we will not be so fervent in our distrust of each other,' he remarked. 'After all, we desire one another, so there is hope that somewhere amongst all the ill feeling there is something that could be more lasting.'

Charlotte wanted to believe him but her only hope was for her name to be cleared. How could he ever develop the feelings he'd had for her before while he still believed her guilty of betraying him in such a despicable way?

Damon brushed a strand of her hair away from her mouth, the touch of his fingers sending a wave of deep longing through her.

'Come to bed, *agape mou*,' he said gently. 'This is the first night of our new life together. We should start it as we mean to go on.'

She moistened her dry lips, her stomach giving a little kick of excitement deep inside. 'Y-you mean… sleep together?'

His eyes darkened as he outlined the curve of her mouth with his fingertip. 'Is that not what husbands and wives do?'

'Yes…but…'

He moved closer, half a step, but it was enough to bring his body into intimate contact with hers. She felt the heat emanating off him, scorching her from the waist down as his desire for her became apparent. She could feel his swollen thickness pressing against her, making her heart begin to race at the thought of feeling him moving inside her.

His mouth descended as she tipped hers upwards, somehow meeting in the middle with an explosion of feeling. His tongue drove through the shield of her lips in search of hers, calling it into a tantalising dance that mimicked the stroke and sensual glide of his physical possession. Her body strained to get closer, her breasts swelling with need as his hands moved over them to shape them possessively.

His kiss deepened with urgency, her lips crushed beneath his as his mouth fed hungrily off hers as if the past three weeks without touching her had driven him to the very limit of his control.

He lifted his mouth from hers as he backed her towards the bed, his eyes glazed with passion. 'It is always this way with you,' he said, his tone rough and deep. 'I only have to touch you and I want to drive myself into you and explode.'

His words fuelled her need of him to fever pitch. She clung to him, her mouth searching for his in desperation as he pressed her to the bed, his long legs entrapping hers. She fought with his clothes in her quest to find his naked skin, her mouth anointing him with hot little kisses as soon as his shirt and trousers were dispensed with.

Damon drew in a sharp-edged little breath as she moved her way down his body to taste him, her tongue a tormenting pleasure as it licked and stroked in turn. He dug his hands into the cloud of her tousled hair as she drew on him, the sucking motion of her mouth lifting every single hair on his scalp in exquisite delight.

He could stand it no longer and pushed her away, his hands taking control of hers by holding them above her head. She squirmed and writhed beneath him as he used his other hand to remove her top so he could caress her breasts, his mouth taking each one in turn until she was whimpering with pleasure.

'Oh, please…' she panted and grabbed at him impatiently as he took his time removing the rest of her clothes.

'Be patient, *agape mou*,' he growled playfully as he kissed his way past her cleavage to her belly button, lingering there a moment to insert the tip of his tongue into the tiny sensitive cave.

She felt him momentarily tense as he came to her Caesarian scar, his eyes coming back to hers with a question in their dark depths. 'You had a difficult birth?' he asked, his tone deep and huskier than normal.

'Yes…I was in labour for twelve hours and Emily was getting distressed…I had to have an emergency Caesarian.'

A shadow of regret flicked in and out of his gaze. 'Was anyone there with you to support you?'

Her breath caught in her throat as his fingers splayed over her belly where his child had lain for nine months. How she had longed for him to be have been present on that day. To encourage her to keep going, to mop her brow and hold her hand through every contraction as it marched back through her abdomen. Hearing that first mewing cry had been one of the happiest and yet loneliest moments of Charlotte's life. She had held that sticky, wriggling little body to her chest and grieved that Damon had not been there to share in the joy and relief of Emily's birth.

'No…' she said, unable to hold his gaze. 'My mother had died three weeks earlier and Stacey… Well, I'm not sure to this day where she was… She'd promised to be with me, but…'

He tipped up her chin to bring her eyes back to his. 'Charlotte…' He seemed to be having trouble speaking, his throat was moving up and down but no further sound came out.

'It's all right,' she said with a tight little smile. 'I had a good midwife and the doctor was wonderful.'

His eyes moved back to her scar and his fingers traced over it gently. 'Did it hurt?' he asked.

'Not as much as the thought of losing her,' she said. 'I would have gone through any pain to avoid that. I still would.'

His expression was thoughtful as he looked deep into her eyes, as if he was seeing her for the very first time.

'You have done well to raise her alone,' he said.

'Thank you...'

He bent his head to reclaim her mouth, the passion rekindling in the first movement of his tongue against hers as his hand moved from her belly to the secret treasure below.

Charlotte let out a tiny gasp as his fingers separated her, her back arching as he stroked the tender nub of aroused flesh that pulsed and flickered with longing.

He lifted his mouth from hers and moved down her body, the intimate invasion of his lips and tongue sending her out of control. She sobbed with the sheer force of her response as it rocketed throughout her body like a thousand miniature earthquakes.

Her breathing was still nowhere near normal when he moved back over her, his weight stabilised by his arms as he entered her with a deep, gliding thrust, his low grunt of satisfaction sending a shivery feeling over her skin.

He drove harder and deeper, carrying her along with him on a fast ride to paradise, the tension building all over again as she matched his rhythm.

His skin was hot and damp on hers, his chest hair an erotic abrasion on the tender swell of her breasts. His strong legs were like a vice holding hers apart for the next deep surge and retreat of his body.

She could feel him approaching the ultimate moment, his breathing beginning to get harder and faster and his body tensing all over, as if poised on a precipitous edge. She lifted her hips slightly but it was enough to tip him over. He gave a deep shuddering groan and spilled himself, the pumping movements against her swollen femininity sending her into oblivion with him.

Charlotte let out a sigh of total relaxation as her body gradually floated back to earth, her eyelids feeling as if they were weighted with anvils as she snuggled into the warmth of his collapsed weight above hers.

'Am I too heavy for you?' he asked against the creamy softness of her neck.

'No…' She gave another little sigh and wrapped her arms around his waist. 'No, you feel wonderful…'

It was a while before Damon realised she had fallen asleep. Her breathing was relaxed and even and her body totally pliant, all except for her arms.

They were holding him as if they never wanted to let him go…

CHAPTER THIRTEEN

As soon as the plane touched down in Athens Charlotte felt her stomach begin to twist and tighten with nerves. It had been a pleasant flight, all things considered. Certainly the luxury of Damon's private jet had more than a little to do with it, but in spite of that she couldn't help noticing a softening of his attitude towards her. He had chatted to her on neutral subjects during the times she had been unable to sleep, his demeanour showing no sign of his earlier anger or resentment. She wondered if it was for the benefit of his attentive staff or whether he was genuinely trying to put the past aside and build a bridge of friendship with her.

Their connecting flight to Santorini was leaving in just under an hour, which meant that she would come face to face with Damon's mother for the first time in four years. She wondered how the older woman would receive her, especially since Charlotte had kept the existence of her only grandchild a secret. She also couldn't help wondering how Damon had explained his hasty marriage. His mother was too astute to be fooled into thinking it was a love match. Alexandrine was close to her son and would soon see for herself the cracks in his relationship with his new wife.

'Are we dere yet?' Emily asked with a sleepy yawn as their luggage was transferred by Damon's staff.

'Not quite, darling,' Charlotte said, cuddling her close. 'We have one more short flight and then you will be able to see your granny.'

Damon met her eyes briefly and he gave her one of his slow smiles. 'Would you like me to hold her for you?' he offered. 'You look tired.'

'OK…thanks…' She handed Emily to him, her hands brushing against his. She felt the exchange of sexual energy and her skin began to tighten all over in reaction.

'My mother will be so thrilled to see Emily,' he said as he stroked his daughter's sleepy head where it was resting against his shoulder. 'You have no need to be concerned over anything else.'

She gnawed at her lip without answering.

'Truly, Charlotte,' he assured her. 'The past is not going to be mentioned while we are here.'

'That doesn't mean it's going to go away,' she said as the flight crew assembled prior to boarding.

Damon watched as she moved towards the boarding gate, her shoulders bowed with exhaustion, her chestnut hair falling in cascading waves about her shoulders, the normally smooth creamy skin of her face now looking pinched and white.

He felt something catch in his chest, like a small sharp tug on the feelings he had locked away four years ago. Although he hadn't told her he had loved her in so many words, her bubbly nature and enthusiasm for life had been so refreshing. She had captivated him from the very first moment their eyes had met across a crowded restaurant. He had felt a connection that had been instant, electric and enthralling and, even now, in spite of what she had done, he could still feel it beating like a pulse deep inside him.

Maybe she was right, he thought as he moved towards the boarding gate with his tiny daughter fast asleep in his arms.

The past was not going to go away.

It would stay with them like a menacing presence, casting a long dark shadow of uncertainty over their lives…

The Latousakis residence was in the traditional settlement of Finikia, just east of the village of Oia, the starkly white-washed buildings in the bright summer sunlight making Charlotte quickly shield her eyes. The inimitable blue of the Aegean Sea sparkled below, the faint smell of donkeys and fish and salt in the air bringing back a host of bitter-sweet memories.

She had arrived on the island four years ago with a backpack and had fallen in love on the second day, and with Damon as her guide had explored all the tourist spots. They had sat and watched what were reputed to be the best sunsets in the world by the Kastro walls, jostling for a position just like everyone else, their smiles only for each other.

They had swum at the tiny port of Ammoudi, and most of the black sand beaches, glorying in the heat of the summer and the fire of their love. He had taught her the language of love and the choreography of mind-blowing sex, all within the space of a few short weeks. She had never been happier; each bright sunny day had been a gift as she had basked in the glorious experience of being adored by a man who was perfect in every way.

It was painful to be back where it had all started. It brought the loss of it all so sharply into focus after years of trying to keep it out of sight and out of mind.

Alexandrine was waiting for them in the doorway, her arms outstretched for Emily who had not long ago woken.

'Are you my granny?'

Charlotte saw the bright tears in Damon's mother's eyes

as she reached for her only grandchild and felt a lump come
to her already tight throat.

'Oh, my darling one,' the older woman crooned, her voice
breaking over the words. 'You are the image of Eleni.'

Damon smiled and bent down to kiss his mother. 'She is a
beautiful child, Mama.'

Alexandrine turned her dark brown eyes to Charlotte, her
expression warm and welcoming. 'It is good to see you,
Charlotte. I am so glad you are here and a part of our family.'

Charlotte found it hard to know what to say in response.
She stretched her lips into a smile and offered a hand but
Alexandrine ignored it to press a soft kiss to both of her
cheeks, with Emily still locked in her embrace.

'It's good to be here again…' she mumbled.

Emily rubbed at her eyes. 'Do you want to see my special
toys?' she asked her grandmother.

Alexandrine's eyes brightened. 'I would love to see your
special toys. Did you bring them all this way with you?'

'Mummy wasn't going to let me, but Daddy said I could,'
Emily said with a borderline reproachful glance in
Charlotte's direction.

'I am sure your mummy was worried about your things
taking up too much room,' Alexandrine said graciously.

'Do you have a swimming pool?' Emily asked as she
slipped her tiny hand into her grandmother's outstretched one.

'Yes, we do.' Alexandrine smiled. 'Would you like to see it?'

Emily turned to Charlotte with a beseeching look. 'Can I,
Mummy?'

Charlotte nodded, her face cracking on a smile. 'Of
course you can.'

'Can you swim?' Emily asked her grandmother as they made
their way through the house to the sun-drenched terrace outside.

'But of course,' Alexandrine replied. 'Can you?'

'Only a little bit,' Emily confessed as her thumb began to move towards her mouth. 'Mummy has been taking me to lessons but I'm not berry good.'

Damon turned to Charlotte once they had gone, his expression softened with concern. 'Are you all right? You look very pale.'

Her body slumped on a sigh. 'I don't know why I feel so exhausted,' she said, rubbing the centre of her forehead. 'Maybe it's the heat.'

'It is certainly a change from what you are used to, although as far as I could tell Sydney was not having a particularly cold winter.'

'Would you mind if I lie down for a while?' she asked.

'Of course not,' he said with another one of his rarely used smiles. 'My mother will relish this opportunity to get to know her granddaughter.'

'If Emily needs me, please wake me up,' Charlotte said a few minutes later when Damon had shown her to their room.

'Do not worry about her,' he said as he pulled a cool sheet over her. 'She will undoubtedly soon crash from jet lag just as you are doing now.'

'I never used to suffer from jet lag,' she said as she brought a hand up to cover her aching eyes. 'I used to trip between time zones without a problem.'

'You have been working hard for the last few weeks,' he reminded her.

'Yes…' Her soft sigh deflated her chest as she nestled into the pillows and closed her eyes. 'I guess you're right… It's been one hell of a month…'

'If you do not feel up to joining us for dinner, do not worry,' he said. 'I can get the housekeeper to bring something up to your room.'

Charlotte felt her stomach shrink away at the thought of

food and buried her head further into the soft-as-air pillow. 'I'm not hungry…'

'My mother is the happiest I have seen her in two years,' he said after a long silence.

She opened her eyes to look at him. 'I'm glad…I really am…'

'The loss of a child is huge in a mother's life,' he said, looking down at his hands for a moment before bringing his dark, unreadable eyes back to hers. 'I hope you will forgive me for threatening to take Emily from you. If things do not work out between us, I will try to ensure she has regular contact with you.'

'Thank you…' she murmured, wondering if she could trust him to keep his word.

'You have been a good mother to her,' he said. 'Do not be hurt by her occasional divided loyalties. It is understandable that she will be trying to work out who is now in charge. Children do that in order to feel secure; there is nothing personal in it, I am sure.'

'I could never afford the toys you've bought for her,' she said, not quite able to remove the hint of resentment in her tone.

He put his hand on her shoulder, the warmth of his palm seeping through her skin like a brand. 'I am only trying to make up for lost time. The things I buy for her are not bribes to win her away from you.'

Charlotte did nothing to hide the cynicism in her eyes as they connected with his. 'I can't compete with overseas holidays and expensive gifts. I can only give her myself.'

His hand dropped from her shoulder as his expression tightened. 'You at least have had that opportunity for the last three years. I have not.'

She buried her head into the pillow, her voice sounding muffled as she spoke. 'Please close the door. I don't want to be disturbed.'

'I do not like it when you turn away from me when I am speaking to you.'

'Get over it.'

She heard his indrawn breath, his anger at her curt dismissal pulsing in the air. 'Look at me, Charlotte,' he commanded.

She flipped over to her back to fling him a frosty look. 'Just because we're married doesn't mean you can order me about all the time. If you wanted a compliant wife, then you should have married someone of your own culture. No doubt they would have sat at your feet licking your boots in subservience. If I don't want to look at you, I won't and there is nothing you can do to make me.'

His eyes flickered with fury at her mutinous glare, his hands in tight knots by his sides as he ground out, 'You are the most maddening woman I have ever met. I am trying to bring about peace in our relationship and yet you consistently resist all of my attempts to effect a truce.'

Her eyes flashed back at him. 'I don't trust you, that's why. For all I know, you could be leading me up the garden path, making me fall in love with you all over again before you snatch Emily away from me.'

'It is not my intention to have you fall in love with me.'

Charlotte felt her anger draining away to make room for her disappointment. She felt it gradually filling her chest until she could scarcely breathe for the weight of it. She fought hard to hide it from him, schooling her features into bland indifference. 'Good, then at least you won't be setting yourself up for disappointment.'

'That is what I figured,' he returned with equal indifference. 'Love would only complicate our situation as it stands. We share the bond of a child and at the moment a lingering attraction that will no doubt burn itself out in time.'

A small frown found its way back to her forehead. 'So what happens then?' she asked.

'We will deal with that when it happens,' he answered evenly.

'Are you talking weeks or months or years?'

His dark eyes were as unfathomable as ever as they held on to hers. 'I would hazard a guess and say it could take some time for me to flush you out of my system.'

She rolled her eyes in disdain. 'You make me sound like some sort of unpleasant stomach virus.'

His mouth stretched into an unwilling smile. 'That is indeed what it feels like at times,' he conceded.

'Yeah, well, you're more or less a major pain in the rear end for me too,' she tossed back.

He was still smiling. 'I will come in later to check on you.'

She turned her head back into the pillow. 'Don't bother.'

'It is no bother; besides, my mother will suspect something is wrong if I do not act like a devoted husband. She is delighted we are together again.'

Charlotte lifted her head out of the downy pillow to look at him. 'Why? Has she suddenly changed her mind about what happened four years ago?'

'This may surprise you, but my mother always found it difficult to believe you were responsible.'

She hunted his expression, hoping for some sign of his own belief in her innocence, but as far as she could tell there was none. The blade of his gaze relentlessly dissected hers until she was the first to look away.

'What a pity she wasn't able to convince you of the same,' she said, looking down at her hands where they were twisting the hem of the sheet covering her.

The silence stretched and stretched until it was finally broken by the slow release of his sigh. 'Yes,' he said as her eyes slowly came back to his. 'Yes, perhaps it is.'

She ran her tongue over the parchment of her lips. 'Damon...'

He reached out with a fingertip and pressed her mouth closed. 'No more talking of the past, Charlotte.'

He gave her a crooked smile and, bending down, replaced his finger with his mouth in a soft brush-like kiss that made her lips cling momentarily to his as he pulled away.

She watched as he moved to the door, the words to call him back locked in the middle of her throat. What would be the point in telling him she loved him? It wasn't what he wanted from her.

Not now.

Not again.

Not ever.

Charlotte opened her eyes during the early hours of the morning to see Damon lying beside her, his deep and even breathing indicating he was sound asleep.

She lay looking at him, her fingers itching to reach out and touch his shadowed jaw, to trace the sensual curve of his mouth and the length of his aristocratic nose.

His legs moved until they were touching hers, her whole body shivering as she felt the rough abrasion of his masculine hair along the silky length of her shins and calves.

His lips moved and a soft breathless sound came out. 'Loula…'

Her eyes widened, her whole body freezing in shock. Her stomach hollowed in anguish as she edged away, her limbs feeling uncoordinated and useless as she got awkwardly out of the bed.

She heard the sound of him moving behind her. 'Charlotte?'

She turned and gave him an acidic glare. 'Yep, that's me. Nice of you to remember my name.'

He eased himself up on one elbow, his brows moving together over his still sleepy eyes. 'What the hell are you talking about?'

She folded her arms crossly. 'You were calling out for your lover.'

He brought a hand up to his jaw and gave it a quick rub. 'Which one?'

Her mouth dropped open. *'You mean there's more than one?'* she choked.

'I am not sure how to answer. You surely did not expect me to be celibate for the past four years?'

She turned away in disgust. 'Please spare me the sordid details of your sexual exploits.'

'You are jealous.'

She swung back around to deny it but the room began to spin alarmingly and she clutched at mid-air to steady herself. 'No…' She tottered for a moment, her eyes trying to focus on something stable, but even the bed seemed to be in motion.

Damon leapt out of bed and reached for her before she toppled forward. 'Here, sit down and put your head between your knees,' he said as he gently directed her back to the bed.

Charlotte did as he said, closing her eyes so she didn't have to cope with the rolling of the floor as well.

'Are you feeling unwell?' he asked.

She groaned as a wave of nausea rose like a swelling tide in her stomach. 'Oh, God…I think I'm going to be sick…'

She only just made it to the *en suite* bathroom in time, before she threw up the meagre contents of her stomach.

Damon rinsed the mess away and, using the basin's twin, quickly rinsed a face cloth and handed it to her.

'I think I should call the doctor,' he said. 'You must have picked up a bug of some sort from the flight.'

Charlotte clutched at the basin as the room began to spin out of control again. She could hear his voice coming at her through a vacuum, the concern in his tone moving further and further away from her. She turned her head sideways to try and bring him back into focus but he was a dark blur. She felt her legs folding, leaving her without support. Even her fingers gradually lost their grip, the tingling of her fingertips making her feel as if shifting grains of sand were beneath her skin instead of flesh and blood.

She felt Damon take her weight as she slipped sideways, her eyelashes struggling to keep open, but the sickening swirl of the bathroom was too much for her. She gave in to the lure of dark oblivion with a soft sigh of resignation…

'How long has she been unwell?'

Charlotte opened her eyes at the sound of the heavily accented voice. She saw Damon standing by the bedside with a man carrying what looked to be a doctor's bag.

'I'm not unwell,' she said, struggling upright. 'I'm fine now…'

Damon pressed her back down gently. 'No, indeed you are not, *agape mou*. Dr Tsoulis will take your temperature at the very least. What you have might be catching. I do not want Emily's first real holiday to be spoilt by illness.'

Charlotte flopped back down. She didn't have the energy to fight him and certainly not in front of the doctor. 'All right, but I can assure you it's just jet lag.'

The doctor took her temperature and gave a shrug. 'No, she is not running a fever,' he said and reached for his portable blood pressure machine.

'I told you I'm perfectly fine.'

'When was your last menstrual period?' the doctor asked as her blood pressure was measured.

Charlotte could feel her face heating under the watchful gaze of Damon. 'Um…I've been a bit irregular lately…'

'Which means we cannot exactly rule out the possibility of pregnancy,' Dr Tsoulis said and reached for a syringe.

Charlotte gulped. 'What are you doing?'

'I would like to run a few blood tests on you as well as a

pregnancy test,' he said as he placed a tourniquet on her arm. 'Fainting is often associated with anaemia. Have you been feeling unusually tired of late?'

'Yes…' She winced as the needle pricked her skin. 'Ouch!'

'I am sorry,' the doctor said, releasing the tourniquet. 'You have small veins.'

He placed a sticky patch on the puncture site and gave her a reassuring smile. 'I am sure this will tell us what we need to know. In the meantime I suggest you get as much rest as you can.'

Damon escorted the doctor out and, after a few minutes, returned with a glass of freshly squeezed orange juice. 'Emily is with my mother,' he informed her. 'She has had breakfast and is keen to go swimming.'

'Doesn't she want to see me?'

'I told her you were resting,' he said. 'I do not want her to worry unnecessarily.'

Charlotte could feel her resentment building. 'I told you I am not sick, Damon.'

'We will not know that until the test results come in.'

'Anaemia is not contagious.'

'You might have any number of things wrong,' he pointed out. 'I would like to play safe until we know for sure.'

'You're doing this deliberately, aren't you?' She sent him an accusing glare. 'You're nudging me out of Emily's life so she won't miss me when you get rid of me for the second time.'

He looked down at her with a brooding expression. 'You are developing a persecution complex. I have no intention of getting rid of you. Our relationship will not end until such time as we both desire it.'

'If you were being truthful you'd admit you'd like to end it right now,' she said. 'So you can get on with your relationship with Loula or whatever her name is.'

'Loula is the housekeeper. I must have heard you moving

and unconsciously thought it was her coming in to change the bed or something.'

'So you've been sleeping with the hired help again?' she said with a scornful look. 'I thought you would have learned from your past mistakes.'

'You have been the only mistake I have made and it is not one I am proud of,' he bit out.

'Gee, thanks,' she tossed back. 'Nice to know I made an impression.'

His eyes went heavenwards as if in search of patience. 'I do not want to argue with you. You are not well.'

'How many times do I have to say I'm fine?'

'I want you to stay in bed for the day.'

She thrust the sheet aside and got out of bed to defy him. 'I will do no such thing.'

Black eyes warred with blue in a fiery challenge that Charlotte knew she had no hope of winning. Her stomach was already churning all over again and her legs wobbling beneath her.

'Get back into bed,' he said.

She pulled back her shoulders. 'No.'

'Get in or I will make you get in.'

'I'd like to see you try.'

'Is that a dare?' he asked.

'No, it's a warning that if you come anywhere near me I will scream.'

He smiled a devilish smile as he stepped closer. 'My mother will assume you are voicing your intense pleasure at being in my arms.'

Charlotte looked for an escape route but the bed was in the way. 'Don't touch me.'

'Why?' he asked with a glint in his black eyes. 'In case you respond?'

'I am not going to respond,' she said but she knew her voice lacked conviction.

'How about we put it to the test?' he suggested, cupping her face with his hand, his warm fingers immediately stoking a fire in her belly.

She swallowed as he closed the distance between their bodies, his thighs brushing against the unsteadiness of hers. 'D-don't do this…' she said on a whisper.

'Don't do what?' he asked, bringing his mouth within a breath of hers. 'This?'

She closed her eyes as his lips brushed hers, the tingling of her mouth beneath the alluring pressure of his sending all thought of resisting him to some far-away unreachable place. His tongue broke the seal of her lips with a hot sensual probe that curled her toes and hollowed out her stomach. She pressed herself against him, her need spreading through her like wildfire. The heat from his mouth on hers fuelled the flames until she was only upright because he was holding her in his steely embrace.

Her tongue flicked against the scorching thrust of his, making her senses instantly soar. Her blood leapt in her veins, her heart starting to pound in time with the throbbing pulse of desire she could feel spreading from deep and low in her belly to the achingly hollow place between her legs.

She could feel his response to her, the hard ridge of his erection swelling against her stomach, and the increasing urgency of his mouth as it devoured hers. His hands moved over her possessively, shaping her breasts before he pushed her clothing aside to gain access to the satin of her skin. Her breath caught in her throat as his mouth moved from hers to suckle each tight nipple in turn until she was reeling from the passionate onslaught.

His dark, triumphant gaze met hers, making Charlotte

realise she was playing right into his hands by responding to him so unreservedly. She gave him a chilly look and rearranged her clothes, pausing for a moment before she lifted her hand to her mouth to wipe away the taste of him.

'Get out,' she said.

His mouth tilted arrogantly. 'You are angry at yourself, not me, *agape mou*,' he said. 'It annoys you that you cannot help yourself, does it not? You respond to me so delightfully every single time.'

She tightened her mouth without answering, her hands going to fists at her sides.

'You are mine, Charlotte,' he said, tethering her to him by a handful of her hair as he brought his mouth back to hers. 'You are mine, body and soul.'

Charlotte fought against her response as his lips commandeered hers, but somehow the hands that had started to push him away were now clinging to his shirt front, her mouth kissing him back with teeth, lips and tongue with an almost savage intent.

She swallowed his deep groan as she wrenched at his shirt, her hands skating over his naked flesh, her nostrils flaring so she could breathe in the clean male scent of him.

She fumbled with his belt and trousers, relishing the sounds of his pleasure as her fingers finally found him, hot and hard and heavy in her hands. She slithered down his body until she was on her knees in front of him, her tongue tasting him in a tiny cat-lick fashion that brought another rough groan from the depths of his throat.

His fingers were still in her hair, bunched against the maelstrom of feeling she was about to unleash. She felt his tension building, his legs braced as she lured him relentlessly to the point of no return.

He shuddered and spilled himself, the sharp one word expletive bursting from his lips indicating to Charlotte that he had not intended to lose control in such a way.

It was a salve to her pride as she straightened to see the somewhat bewildered expression on his face. She watched as he refastened his trousers, a dull flush running underneath the olive tone of his jaw.

'I am sorry,' he said, shoving a hand through his hair.

'It's fine.'

His frown deepened. 'Charlotte…'

'It's OK, Damon,' she said airily in an effort to disguise how deeply affected she was. 'I was getting my own back.'

He gave her a puzzled look. 'What do you mean?'

She lifted her chin. 'You think I have no self-control where you are concerned. I wanted to demonstrate that you are really no better.'

'I have never denied my attraction for you.'

She gave him a brittle glance. 'No, that's definitely true.'

His expression clouded again. 'Look, Charlotte, I have tried to make amends for how I treated you.'

'How? By forcing me into a loveless marriage so you can have full access to your child?'

'Marriage was the only option I could take. My mother is somewhat progressive in her outlook compared to other women of her generation, but I am a high profile person in a relatively close community. I would be looked upon with disdain for not marrying the mother of my child.'

'Even though you hate me?'

'Those are your words, not mine.'

'You don't need to say a word, your actions are more than loud enough,' she said.

A taut silence throbbed between them.

'Have you heard from your sister recently?' he finally asked.

A small, barely audible sigh escaped from her lips. 'No…'

'Then you will be pleased to know she is doing remarkably well.'

Charlotte began to gape at him. 'Wh-what do you mean?'

'I had a meeting with Stacey and I gave her an ultimatum. It was either clean up or be locked up. She decided a stint in a private detox clinic paid for by me was better than several months incarcerated in prison.'

Her eyes widened in amazement, her heart leaping with hope. 'She's really going ahead with it?'

He nodded. 'I have left someone in charge to make sure she stays the distance. She has been there nearly three weeks.'

'But why didn't you tell me until now?'

He gave her an enigmatic look as he reached for the door. 'I was getting my own back, Charlotte. Although three weeks is hardly as long as four years, is it?'

She opened her mouth to answer, but he had already gone.

CHAPTER FOURTEEN

'MUMMY look at me!' Emily called to Charlotte from the pool on the terrace outside a few days later. 'I'm swimming!'

Charlotte smiled as her little daughter flung her body towards her beaming grandmother, her tiny arms and legs thrashing at the sparkling water.

Alexandrine gathered Emily close as she came up for air. 'Why do you not join us, Charlotte?' she asked.

'Yes, Mummy, come in and I'll show you what else I can do,' Emily piped up excitedly.

Charlotte slipped off her sarong and slipped into the cool embrace of the water with a sigh of pure pleasure.

'How are you feeling today?' Alexandrine asked after Emily had bobbed under the surface to show off her bubble-blowing.

'Much better,' Charlotte said. 'I think I'm finally over my jet lag.'

'You still look a little fragile,' Alexandrine said. 'Damon is concerned about you.'

Charlotte focused her gaze on her daughter rather than meet the older woman's eyes. 'He's been very kind,' she said with complete honesty.

She still couldn't quite believe he had taken control of Stacey's problems so effectively. She had finally been able to speak to her sister, who'd assured her she was making good progress. It touched Charlotte very deeply that he had done everything in his power to pull Stacey back from the brink. She couldn't make sense of his motives, for while he had made love to her each night, he had revealed nothing of his feelings. It felt as if hope and dread were constantly jostling for space in her chest.

'Emily has made him so happy,' Alexandrine said. 'And me too, of course.' She released a little sigh and added, 'Every time I look at her I see a glimpse of Eleni.'

Emily popped back up, her brown eyes dancing with excitement. 'Did you see me, Mummy? Even Janie can't do dat!'

Charlotte pressed a soft kiss to her daughter's little button nose. 'You are very clever but I think you have a very good teacher in your granny. She is much more patient than me.'

'Patience is something I have had to learn the hard way,' Alexandrine confessed once Emily had scampered off to play with her toys in the shade by the pool. 'Every day is a challenge not to be angry at God for what has been taken away from me.'

Charlotte turned to look at her mother-in-law. 'I can't tell you how sorry I was to hear of your loss. You must miss Eleni dreadfully.'

'It has been so hard,' the older woman said, her eyes filming with tears. 'But you have given me such a gift in Emily. I could not believe it when Damon called to say he had found you at last and that you had had his child.'

'I tried to tell him, but—'

Alexandrine put a hand on her arm. 'Please do not apologise. He was so angry back then and far too stubborn for his own good. I told him there could have been another explanation but he would not hear of it.'

Charlotte wanted to reiterate her innocence but Emily

was coming back towards the pool, this time with Damon holding her hand.

'Daddy's going to swim with me,' she announced proudly.

Charlotte felt the sweep of Damon's gaze as he entered the water close to her, the rippling waves his large body set off brushing against her breasts as if he had reached out and touched her.

'You finally have some colour in your cheeks,' he observed, as his thigh brushed against hers beneath the screen of the water.

She began to turn away but encountered a contemplative look from her mother-in-law and turned straight back and smiled up at him. 'I feel wonderful.'

His eyes blazed with intense heat as they roved over the up-thrust of her breasts in her bikini top. 'You certainly look wonderful.'

'Emily and I are going inside,' Alexandrine called out diplomatically.

Damon sent his mother a grateful glance before meeting Charlotte's flustered look. 'It looks like we are alone again, *agape mou*,' he drawled silkily.

She backed against the wall of the pool, her breathing escalating. 'Don't even think about it.'

He pressed closer, his aroused length probing the quivering jelly of her belly. 'No one will see us.'

'Th-that's completely beside the point.'

He ran his hands lightly down her arms. 'You are shaking, Charlotte.'

'I'm getting cold.'

'You feel hot to me.'

She ran her tongue over her lips, trying to put some distance between them, but he wasn't allowing it. She could feel every ridge and plane of his body until she was uncertain of where she ended and he began.

She watched in mesmerised fascination as his mouth came down, her eyelashes fluttering closed at the first whisper of warmth over the tingling surface of her lips. She felt the subtle probe of his tongue seeking entry and her lips parted on a deep sigh of pleasure, her stiff limbs loosening as soon as he took control of her mouth.

Her breasts swelled and ached for his attention, her inner core contracting in anticipation of his surging presence.

He reached down to cup her tender mound, his fingers sliding into her with a deftness that stole her breath and heightened her excitement. She pushed against him greedily, wanting more of his exquisite touch, uncaring that they were in full view of the villa.

Before she knew what was happening, he had lifted her from the water to settle her on the edge of the pool, stepping into the silky embrace of her open thighs.

'No…not here…' She made a vain effort to stop him, but it was too late. He had already uncovered her to anoint her with his mouth and tongue while her fingers dug into his scalp to anchor herself against the torrent of feeling she knew was just seconds away.

She felt herself lift off, the rush of sensations overloading her until she couldn't think of anything but how he was making her feel. Wave after wave of rapture rolled over her, leaving her spent and useless.

She opened her eyes once the storm was over, hot colour seeping into her cheeks. 'You shouldn't have done that.'

His black eyes glinted. 'I had a score to settle from the other night.'

'You could have chosen a less public venue,' she said with a reproachful look.

'Ah, yes, but we have an audience who need convincing

that this is a real marriage. What better way to demonstrate it than my uncontrollable desire for you and yours for me?'

'I hardly think we have to go to such extremes as this.'

'I will go to whatever extremes I consider necessary,' he said.

She sent him a blistering glare. 'I don't want Emily to see us pawing at each other like animals. It's disgusting.'

He smiled as he ran a hand down the length of her arm, his fingers encircling her wrist like a steel bracelet. 'It is not disgusting, *agape mou*, what is between us. We cannot make it go away by ignoring it. We want each other like a drug. Your sister's addiction is nothing to ours. Four years of detox has done nothing to quell my need for you. I want you as much, if not more than the first time I met you.'

'You want access to your daughter,' she said. 'Don't let's cloud the issue with insincere sentimentality.'

'I want my daughter in my life but I also want you.'

'For now.'

He frowned at the downward turn of her mouth. 'You sound disappointed.'

'I'm not.' Charlotte knew she had answered far too quickly. She could see it in his eyes as they studiously assessed hers.

'My mother has invited guests this evening,' he informed her after a small pause. 'Iona and her husband, Nick Andreakos, will be joining us for dinner. My mother is keen to show off her granddaughter; I hope you do not mind.'

'Why should I mind?' she said, affecting a disinterested tone.

'I just thought you should know.'

'Thank you for telling me. I'll make sure I brush off my besotted bride smile so it sparkles convincingly.'

He trailed a fingertip down the creamy curve of her cheek, coming so close to her mouth she could feel her lips tingling all over again. 'You do that, *agape mou*,' he said. 'Who knows who might be watching?'

* * *

Charlotte heard the guests arriving later that evening but purposely stalled in order to get control of her nerves. She took her time dressing and applying a small amount of make-up, trying not to notice the shadows both in and underneath her eyes.

'Charlotte?' Damon opened the door after the briefest of knocks. 'Iona and Nick have arrived.'

'I'll be down in a minute.'

He closed the door behind him. 'I will wait for you.'

She put down her eyeliner. 'They're here to see Emily, not me.'

'You can hardly hide yourself away indefinitely; besides, Emily is asking for you. She is getting tired and insists on you putting her to bed once she spends a few minutes with our guests.'

Charlotte accompanied him downstairs, a false smile plastered to her face as they entered the sitting room.

'Ah, here she is now,' Alexandrine said with a smile. 'Nick, this is my daughter-in-law, Charlotte. Charlotte, you remember Iona, don't you?'

Charlotte's gaze moved from the warmth of Nick Andreakos's to the cool reception of his wife's. 'Hello, Iona, congratulations on your marriage,' she said politely, trying to chip away at the ice.

'You too,' Iona replied stiffly.

'Mummy?' Emily came trotting over with a huge grin on her face. 'Look what Uncle Nick and Auntie Iona gave me!'

Charlotte looked at the beautiful baby doll in her daughter's arms. 'Wow, isn't that a gorgeous baby?' she said, bending down to Emily's level. 'What have you called her?'

Emily rolled her tiny lips together before looking up at her father for inspiration. 'What do you fink, Daddy? Do you know any good names?'

Damon gave her a tender smile. 'How about we talk about it while I put you to bed, hmm?'

'Is Mummy coming to tuck me in too?'

'Of course,' he said as he scooped her up in his arms. 'Say goodnight, little one.'

Emily smiled shyly and gave the guests a tiny up and down movement of her fingers. 'Night.'

Charlotte excused herself and followed Damon out of the room, but it wasn't until Emily was tucked in and asleep before he addressed a single word to her.

'Iona seems to be a little cold towards you.'

'Yes, well, I did snatch her intended husband away from her four years ago,' she said. 'Perhaps she thinks I might have a go at her new one—Nick.'

He frowned at her tone. 'Do not take too much notice,' he said. 'She is newly pregnant and no doubt feeling a bit touchy.'

'Don't worry,' she assured him brusquely. 'I do know how to conduct myself. I too was pregnant once, you know.'

His eyes held hers for a pulsing moment.

'Are you currently using any form of contraception?' he asked.

She lowered her eyes and began to twist her hands together. 'Um...'

'Is that a yes or a no?'

'It's an I sometimes forget to take my pills regularly,' she confessed as she met his probing look. She nipped at her bottom lip before adding, 'I take a low dose pill to keep my periods in some sort of order. They went out of whack after Emily was born but I'm not very good at remembering to take them. I restarted them when we...you know...'

His eyes were suddenly very dark and intense. 'Has it occurred to you that you might be carrying my child?'

She found it hard to hold his gaze. 'I'm sure I'm not.'

'We have had unprotected sex several times and the pill might not have worked in time.'

'It doesn't necessarily mean I've conceived.'

'Dr Tsoulis will no doubt be able to verify it one way or the other. I have asked him to call me as soon as he gets the results of the tests he ordered.'

Her expression took on an ironic twist. 'I am the person he should be contacting, not you.'

'You are my wife and therefore my responsibility. If you have a health issue, including pregnancy, then I want to be the first to hear of it, not the last.'

Charlotte wanted to argue the point but she could tell by the set of his jaw it would be a wasted effort. She could see the glitter of bitterness in his dark eyes at being shut out of his child's life before.

'I don't want to be pregnant,' she said, but as soon as the words came out of her mouth she regretted them.

'That is a lousy form of contraception,' he said as he held the door for her. 'Wishing and hoping just do not cut it, I am afraid.'

'I meant not yet…'

His eyes bored their way into hers. 'Are you saying you will consider it?'

'I would like things to be more stable between us.'

'We *are* married.'

'That's not enough.'

'What do you want from me, Charlotte?' he asked.

She brought her gaze back to his, her vulnerability on show for the first time. 'I want you to care for me like you did in the past.'

The seconds ticked by heavily as he stood looking down at her, his face an expressionless mask.

'I do not think I am capable of such feeling any more,' he said.

'Because you don't trust me?' she asked.

He stroked a fingertip down the curve of her cheek. 'I think it is myself I do not trust, *agape mou*,' he said with a cryptic smile.

She grasped at his hand and held it tightly in hers. 'Damon…I want you to know I have never stopped loving you.'

She could see his surprise and suspicion having a drawn-out boxing match in his eyes, but it was clear that suspicion won the final round.

'We have guests to entertain,' he said as he pulled his hand out of her hold. 'They will be wondering what has become of us.'

What has become of us, indeed? Charlotte wondered sadly as they walked in silence down the stairs…

CHAPTER FIFTEEN

IT WAS a long drawn out dinner and for every minute of it Charlotte was conscious of Iona's gaze flicking warily to hers. She did her best to ignore it at first but after a while she started to resent the way the other woman was assaulting her with her repeated glances.

'What do you think, Charlotte?' Nick Andreakos suddenly addressed a comment to her but she was lost for an answer.

'I'm sorry…' She gave him an apologetic smile. 'I was miles away. What did you ask?'

'Nick asked if you had considered moving to Santorini permanently,' Damon said with a very direct look.

'I…I don't…I'm not…I…'

Nick smiled. 'I can see she hasn't quite made up her mind, Damon. You will have to work harder to convince her to make her home with you here.'

'It is no matter,' Damon said. 'We can divide our time between Australia and Greece until Emily is of school age. Then we will by necessity have to put down some roots.'

'Would you excuse me?' Charlotte pushed out her chair.

Damon got to his feet. 'Are you all right?' he asked with a dark frown of concern interrupting his features.

She nodded even though it made her already tight head

ache unbearably. 'I'm just feeling a little light-headed. I need some fresh air. I'll be back in a minute.'

Iona got to her feet. 'I will come with you,' she said with a strained smile. 'I need to stretch my legs.'

Charlotte wasn't sure she was in need of company, especially that of a woman who apparently found her presence so distasteful.

'Your daughter is beautiful,' Iona said into the stiff silence as they traversed the marble hall to the main bathroom. 'She is the image of Eleni at that age.'

'Thank you…'

The bathroom door closed behind them and Iona leaned against it, her shoulders suddenly seeming too heavy for her slight frame. 'Charlotte…' she began uncertainly. 'I need to talk to you but it must go no further.'

Charlotte drew in a cautious breath. 'I see…'

'No, you do not,' Iona said. 'You have no idea what I am going to say, do you?'

Charlotte decided to take a wild guess. 'You're going to tell me you were responsible for planting the sculptures in my bag and at the hostel four years ago, right?'

'Wrong.'

Charlotte blinked at her. 'It wasn't you?'

Iona shook her head. 'It was Eleni.'

'Eleni?' She felt her stomach drop. 'But why?'

Iona let out her breath in a jagged stream. 'She did it to protect me. She thought I was in love with her brother. I suppose you know our families had more or less arranged our future union.'

'Yes, I knew about that…'

Iona's dark eyes met hers once more. 'I should have told Eleni the truth, but I was too afraid.'

Charlotte frowned in confusion. 'The truth?'

'I have always loved Damon,' Iona said. 'But like a brother. We had spent most of our childhood together and it was assumed we would make a match of it, but I was not *in* love with him. I was never in love with him. The truth is I have been in love with Nick since I was about twelve; I just wasn't game enough to tell anyone, not even Eleni.'

Charlotte swallowed. 'I don't know what to say.'

'It grieves me terribly to think you have been separated from Damon for all this time because of a silly prank on his sister's part. When I heard you had had his child I was sick with worry. I could barely look at you tonight without being reminded of how your lives have been changed.'

'He doesn't love me.'

'How do you know that?'

Charlotte gave her a bleak look. 'He told me.'

'I do not believe that.'

'He only married me because of Emily.'

Iona's face clenched like a tightened fist. 'It is my fault. I should have said something earlier but I did not want to betray Eleni. She would have hated her mother and brother to think she had acted so childishly and irresponsibly.' She pushed herself away from the door to pace the floor between the mirrored basins. 'I should have come forward earlier but I made a promise.'

'It's all right…'

Iona swung back around to face her. 'It is *not* all right. You are the mother of Damon's child. Don't you see how difficult this is for all of us now?'

Charlotte looked at her without speaking.

'Eleni thought you would go away and never come back, leaving the path open for me to marry her brother,' Iona went on sadly. 'I should have been honest with her from the start. She was so proud of what she had done.'

'I thought she liked me...'

'She did,' Iona said. 'She thought you were wonderful. But she was caught up in her childish dream, that we would become sisters through marriage... Instead we have become separated by death and deceit.'

Charlotte closed her eyes for a moment, trying to make sense of all she had heard.

'Apart from planting the sculptures in your things, Eleni told the boys at the hostel to pretend they had slept with you,' Iona said into the silence. 'I didn't find out until much later she had gone that far. She only confessed that the day she died.'

'So no one knows about this, apart from you?'

Iona shook her head grimly. 'So many times I've wanted to say something to Alexandrine or Damon, but how can I? By doing so I would be destroying their precious memories of Eleni. She begged me on her deathbed never to tell. I haven't even told Nick.'

'But it's destroyed my life,' Charlotte felt the need to point out. 'Damon's too, when it comes to that.'

Iona came closer and grasped her hands in hers. 'No, that is not true. You have won him back. He has married you and you have had his child. He will come to love you again, I am sure. He was in love with you before and will be again.'

Charlotte gave her a smile touched with sadness. 'I wish I had your confidence.'

'He is a good man, Charlotte,' she said. 'He loves his daughter. You have given him such a gift. Do not give up hope.'

'He's never going to find out the truth though, is he?' she asked. 'You won't tell him and I cannot for he won't believe me; he has never believed me.'

Iona's brow furrowed. 'I made a promise to Eleni...'

'Eleni is dead but I am alive. Surely that takes precedence?'

'No.' Iona shook her head. 'I cannot betray my closest friend.'

'She's dead, Iona. She won't hold it against you,' Charlotte said in rising desperation.

A curtain came down over the Greek woman's expression. 'No. I will not do it.'

'Fine.' Charlotte turned away in disgust.

'If it is any comfort, Charlotte, I really like you,' Iona said. 'I liked you from the first time I met you. I know I did not show it; I was trying to put everyone off the scent of my infatuation with Nick by pretending to be put out by your involvement with Damon. But the truth is I have always thought you were perfect for Damon. He needs someone like you, someone strong enough to stand up to him. I knew from an early age I wasn't that person. Do not misunderstand me, Nick is not weak. He is a strong man but he hasn't the ruthless drive of Damon. Damon will stop at nothing to get what he wants, but perhaps you already know that.'

Charlotte turned back to give her a jaded smile. 'I sure do.'

'Please forgive Eleni,' Iona said. 'She thought she was doing the right thing at the time. She would have been devastated to know how much you have been hurt.'

'And yet you will not alleviate that hurt now by telling all to Damon.'

'I cannot do it!' Iona insisted. 'She was my closest friend. Besides, think of how it would hurt Alexandrine to hear of what her daughter did. She is only just coming to terms with her loss, Damon too. Tainting their memories of Eleni with this would be unforgivable.'

Charlotte let out her breath in a stuttered stream. 'No…I guess you're right. It wouldn't do to burst Damon and Alexandrine's bubble right now.'

'Emily is doing a power of good,' Iona said. 'I have not seen Alexandrine smile for months and yet in the company of your little girl she beams from ear to ear.'

'Do you think there will ever be a time when I can clear my name?' Charlotte asked.

Iona gave her a long and studied look. 'I think Damon will come to that realisation himself, if he hasn't already. Besides, wouldn't it be better for him to believe you because he has come to trust you rather than because someone proved your innocence?'

Charlotte could see the sense in Iona's point, even though she desperately wanted to be cleared of any wrongdoing.

'I saw the way he looks at you, as if he cannot quite believe you are back in his life,' Iona continued. 'He might not be ready to admit to his feelings, but he definitely feels something.' She paused delicately and then asked, 'Forgive my asking such a personal question, but is your marriage a physical one?'

Charlotte could feel her cheeks answering for her even as she mumbled in the affirmative.

Iona gave a satisfied smile. 'I thought so. You have a certain glow about you. Is there any chance you could already be pregnant?'

Charlotte nibbled at her bottom lip before answering. 'I don't think so.'

'A baby would be wonderful for you and Damon right now. I am three months gone and I cannot believe how close it has made Nick and I.'

'We should get back to dinner,' Charlotte said. 'Thank you for telling me about Eleni. I realise it must have been hard for you, keeping it to yourself for so long.'

'I wish I could do more for you, Charlotte, but I could not live with myself if I broke my promise to Eleni. It was the very last thing she said to me before she died. She begged me to keep her actions a secret.' She gave her a searching look. 'You do understand, don't you?'

Charlotte let out a tiny sigh. 'I understand,' she said, even though she wasn't entirely sure she did.

Damon turned to Charlotte once the guests had left and his mother had retired to her room. 'Would you like a nightcap?'

'No… I'm pretty tired. I think I'll go straight to bed.'

'You handled this evening very well,' he said. 'I was worried that Iona was going to make a scene. She was sending you some rather strange looks to begin with. What did you talk about when you left the room during dinner?'

'Nothing much, just girl stuff.'

'Nick has been worried about her for weeks,' he said. 'She has apparently been on edge ever since she heard about us meeting up again.'

Charlotte avoided his eyes. 'I expect she wondered if I had changed.'

'In what way?'

She gave a little shrug. 'Who knows? Perhaps she was watching to see if I was going to pilfer the family silver or something.'

He stood watching her for so long that Charlotte began to feel her heart pound in the silence.

'Iona knows nothing about the sculptures,' he said.

'Eleni was her best friend,' she said, mentally kicking herself. 'Perhaps they discussed it some time.'

He shook his head. 'No. Eleni gave me her word she would not tell anyone. I cannot believe she would have let me down in such a way.'

'Lucky you to have such a devoted and trustworthy sister,' she remarked with a touch of irony.

Damon frowned. 'What is that supposed to mean?'

She turned to look at him. 'Do we have to talk about this now?'

'Yes, we do,' he said. 'Have you some reason to believe Eleni spoke to Iona about this?'

Charlotte couldn't think of a way to answer without breaking her promise to Iona. She stood in silence, feeling the burning heat of his dark eyes as they probed her soul.

'Answer me, Charlotte.'

'I would like to go to bed.'

'You will go to bed when I say you can.'

She threw him a defiant glare. 'Don't push me too far, Damon,' she warned him, her voice rising in anger. 'I've had just about enough of your caveman tactics.'

'You only defy me to get me to subdue you,' he said. 'You like to goad me into losing control. I can see the challenge in your eyes.'

'What you can see is my dislike of you.'

He had the gall to smile. 'So the love you confessed to me earlier has suddenly been downgraded to dislike. I knew you were lying. You wanted me to confess similar feelings so you could ridicule them.'

'That's not true!'

His dark eyes glinted cynically. 'I know how your mind works, Charlotte. It would be the ultimate revenge, would it not, for you to hear me confess my love for you, only to reject me as I once did to you.'

'Unlike you, I don't have such a ruthless disregard for people's feelings,' she threw back. 'Don't judge me by your own appalling standards.'

There was a sound at the doorway and Charlotte turned to see Emily standing there with a bundle of bed linen almost as tall as her gathered in her arms, her bottom lip trembling. 'I did a wee-wee in my bed...'she said and began to cry.

'Oh, darling.' Charlotte rushed to her and held her close. 'Don't worry about it. I'll get you some new sheets and pyjamas.'

Emily's little shoulders shook with sobs. 'I heard you fighting with Daddy,' she said. 'He won't stay with us if you're angry at him. Dat's what happened to Janie's daddy. He went away.'

Guilt knifed through Charlotte as she encountered Damon's gaze over the top of Emily's head. 'We're not really fighting,' she said soothingly. 'It was more of a discussion, really.'

'You were shouting,' Emily said with a little sniff as her thumb crept up to her mouth. 'I heard you.'

Damon crouched down to his daughter's level and hitched up her tiny wobbling chin. 'You are right, little one. We were fighting, but it is over now. It is normal for adults to sometimes disagree, but as long as they say sorry, no harm is done.'

'Are you going to say sorry?' Emily asked with big crystal tears still clinging to her sooty lashes.

He smiled at her tenderly and brushed a tear off her tiny cheek with the pad of his thumb. 'Of course I am, little one.'

Emily gave another little sniff, her tiny chest rising and falling with the effort to control her sobs. 'Now?'

He immediately straightened and turned to Charlotte. 'I am sorry for being so pig-headed and arrogant. You do not deserve to be spoken to like that,' he said. 'Will you forgive me?'

Charlotte swallowed against the ridge of emotion in her throat. He had sounded so sincere. If only he really meant it.

'Of course I forgive you…' she mumbled self-consciously.

'Mummy always kisses me when she says sorry,' Emily said. 'Don't you, Mummy?'

'Er…yes…'

'Then I had better kiss Mummy so she knows my apology is genuine,' Damon said. 'What do you think, Emily?'

'I think that's a berry good idea,' Emily said with a beaming smile.

Charlotte tensed as Damon's arms came around her but as

soon as his mouth brushed against hers she felt her whole
body soften. Her eyes closed on a little sigh of pleasure as his
lips came back for another whispering touch, her arms
snaking around his neck, her hips pressing against his where
she could feel his blood quickening.

It took an effort but somehow she managed to step back
from him and reach for her daughter's hand. 'Come on,
Emily,' she said. 'Let's get you into some fresh things so you
can go back to sleep.'

'I don't have to wear a nappy again, do I?' Emily asked as
Charlotte gathered up the bed linen. 'I'm too big to wear one.
You said I am.'

'No, of course not, poppet,' she said, stooping to pick up
a trailing edge of the sheet.

'I will see to these,' Damon said, stepping forward. 'You
change Emily while I bring some fresh linen to her room.'

Charlotte felt the brush of his hand against her breast as he
took the linen from her arms. 'Thank you,' she said, briefly
meeting his eyes.

He smiled a slow smile that warmed his coal-black gaze. 'We
should have done this much earlier,' he said in a low, deep tone.

She gave him a puzzled look. 'What do you mean?'

'Forgiven each other,' he said. 'It is about time, don't you
think?'

She couldn't quite hold his look. 'I forgave you years
ago, Damon,' she said softly as she turned and led Emily
from the room.

CHAPTER SIXTEEN

DAMON was waiting for her in their bedroom when she came in from settling Emily back down. He unfolded himself from the chair he'd been sitting on and came to stand in front of her.

'Charlotte, I meant what I said in front of Emily. I meant every word.'

She stood uncertainly before him, her eyes skittering away from his. 'Thank you…'

He pushed a hand through his hair, which by its disordered state seemed to suggest he had been doing little else for the whole time she had been tucking Emily back into bed. His expression looked pained, as if he was having some trouble formulating what he was about to say.

'I think it is time for us to have a discussion about our future,' he said. 'We cannot continue with this animosity between us. It is affecting Emily. This bed-wetting episode is an indicator of how much she needs us to learn to love and respect each other.'

'Damon, I—'

'No,' he said, cutting her off. 'Please let me continue. I have been rehearsing this for the last few minutes, ever since I realised that I still love you.'

Charlotte blinked at him, wondering if she'd heard him correctly. 'What did you say?'

He gave her a rueful smile. 'I love you, Charlotte. I think it is quite possible I have loved you from the first moment I met you, but back then I was too proud to admit it. I had responsibilities and expectations on me. I could not see any way out of them. When the sculptures were found in your bag and room at the hostel it gave me an out. It gave me a perfect excuse to bring our relationship to an end, even though I really did not want to let you go. But I felt I had to in order to do the right thing by my family. I let my anger blind me to the very real possibility that someone else was responsible for those thefts, someone much closer to home.'

Charlotte unconsciously held her breath.

'You see, Charlotte,' he continued, 'you were the one person who was jeopardising my future, or so someone close to me thought. I am surprised I did not see it earlier, but it was something you said the other night that made me realise how far some people will go to protect those they love. You, for instance, were prepared to agree to my insulting demands of you in order to protect your sister and Emily. It made me realise that my sister could very well have done the same. She desperately wanted Iona to be her sister-in-law. She talked of it a great deal, even up until the time she died, begging me to marry her best friend, even though as time went on I could see it was not what Iona wanted. And, coward that I was, I did not have the heart to tell Eleni it was not what I wanted either. I let her die thinking I was going to do as she had hoped. Of course, knowing Iona as I do, she would have been reluctant to dash Eleni's hopes as well, especially when we all knew Eleni's time was limited. I suspect Iona too allowed my sister to maintain her dream to the very last.'

'Does your mother know about any of this?' she asked.

'I have not wanted to taint her memories of Eleni,' he confessed. 'But sometimes I wonder if she has come to the same conclusion I have.'

'Which is?'

He reached for her hands and held them within the warmth and strength of his, his dark eyes glistening with moisture, his voice rough with emotion. 'I was a fool to let you go four years ago. I should have fought to clear your name. You are incapable of such a betrayal of trust. You are loyal and loving to all who come into your life. The way you love your sister in spite of what she has done shames me. Your belief in her is unshakable. I would have given up long ago, but instead each time she let you down you found new reserves inside yourself to forgive. I can only hope in time you will find it in yourself to forgive me.'

'I told you just a short time ago that I forgave you years ago,' she said with a tiny catch in her voice. 'Didn't you believe me?'

His eyes glistened even more and his throat moved up and down as he fought for control. 'This is four years too late, *agape mou*, but yes, I do believe you.'

Charlotte couldn't control the tears spilling from her eyes. 'I love you so much,' she choked as she clung to him. 'There wasn't a day while we were apart that I didn't think of you.'

'I thought of you too,' he said. 'That is why, when the museum contacted me about the exhibition, I felt it was too good a chance to miss. I just wanted to see you again, to make absolutely sure you were as guilty as I had thought. Seeing you that night made me realise my attraction for you had not gone away. Your response to me made me determined to have you again. Of course, when your sister stole my wallet and I later found it in your bag, I immediately assumed you were up to your old tricks again. I was ruthlessly determined to have my revenge.'

'I was so torn,' she said, looking up at him. 'I wanted to protect Stacey so she could get the help she needed, but I was terrified if you found out about Emily you would take her away from me.'

His expression clouded with remorse. 'I am ashamed of what I threatened,' he said. 'You are the most wonderful mother to our little daughter. It would have been nothing short of cruelty to separate her from you or you from her. We are a family now.'

'A family…' Charlotte breathed the words in wonder.

'Yes,' he said. 'You and me and Emily—the three of us. For now.'

Her blue eyes twinkled up at him. 'For now?'

He gave her a dangerously sexy smile as he brought his mouth close to hers. 'Give me time, *agape mou*. It takes time to build a family.'

'Take all the time you want,' Charlotte said on a breathless little sigh as his mouth finally claimed hers.

EPILOGUE

'WHAT do you think of him?' Charlotte asked as Stacey cradled her tiny newborn nephew in her arms.

'He's perfect…' Stacey breathed in amazement. 'He's so absolutely perfect.'

'We think so, don't we, Charlotte?' Damon said proudly as he put his arm around his wife's shoulders.

'Of course we do, but then we're totally biased,' she said with an adoring look as she met his dark tender gaze.

'Can I have a hold of him now?' Emily bounced up and down impatiently. 'You promised I could after Auntie Stacey had a turn.'

Stacey turned to her sister and smiled shyly. 'And promises should always be kept, right, Charlie?'

Charlotte's smile lit up the room as she looked at her glowing-with-health sister. 'Damon and I want you to be Aleksandar's godmother. Would you do us the honour?'

Stacey's clear blue eyes filmed with tears of joy. 'You just try and stop me,' she said.

QUEENS *of* R♥MANCE

The world's favorite romance writers

New and original novels you'll treasure forever from
internationally bestselling Presents authors, such as:

Lynne Graham
Lucy Monroe
Penny Jordan
Miranda Lee

and many more.

Don't miss
THE GUARDIAN'S
FORBIDDEN MISTRESS
by Miranda Lee
Book #2701

Look out for more titles from your favorite
Queens of Romance, coming soon!

www.eHarlequin.com

HP12701

I ♥

HARLEQUIN *Presents*

BROUGHT TO YOU BY FANS OF
HARLEQUIN PRESENTS.

We are its editors and authors
and biggest fans—and we'd
love to hear from YOU!

Subscribe today to our online blog at
www.iheartpresents.com

HPBLOG

HARLEQUIN *Presents*

┏━━━━━━━━━━━━━━━━━━━━━━━━━┓

The Rich, the Ruthless and the Really Handsome

┗━━━━━━━━━━━━━━━━━━━━━━━━━┛

How far will they go to win their wives?

A trilogy by Lynne Graham

Prince Rashad of Bakhar, heir to a desert kingdom;
Leonidas Pallis, scion of one of Greece's leading dynasties
and Sergio Torrente, an impossibly charismatic,
self-made Italian billionaire.

Three men blessed with power, wealth and looks—
what more can they need? Wives, that's what…and
they'll use whatever means to get them!

THE GREEK TYCOON'S DEFIANT BRIDE

by Lynne Graham

Book #2700

Maribel was a shy virgin when she was bedded by impossibly
handsome Greek tycoon Leonidas Pallis. But when Maribel
conceives his child, Leonidas will claim her…as his bride!

**Don't miss the final installment of Lynne Graham's
dazzling trilogy! Available next month:**

THE ITALIAN BILLIONAIRE'S PREGNANT BRIDE

Book #2707

www.eHarlequin.com

HP12700

REQUEST YOUR FREE BOOKS!

2 FREE NOVELS
PLUS 2
FREE GIFTS!

YES! Please send me 2 FREE Harlequin Presents® novels and my 2 FREE gifts. After receiving them, if I don't wish to receive any more books, I can return the shipping statement marked "cancel." If I don't cancel, I will receive 6 brand-new novels every month and be billed just $3.80 per book in the U.S., or $4.47 per book in Canada, plus 25¢ shipping and handling per book and applicable taxes, if any*. That's a savings of close to 15% off the cover price! I understand that accepting the 2 free books and gifts places me under no obligation to buy anything. I can always return a shipment and cancel at any time. Even if I never buy another book from Harlequin, the two free books and gifts are mine to keep forever.

106 HDN EEXK 306 HDN EEXV

Name _____ (PLEASE PRINT) _____

Address _____ Apt. # _____

City _____ State/Prov. _____ Zip/Postal Code _____

Signature (if under 18, a parent or guardian must sign) _____

Mail to the **Harlequin Reader Service®:**
IN U.S.A.: P.O. Box 1867, Buffalo, NY 14240-1867
IN CANADA: P.O. Box 609, Fort Erie, Ontario L2A 5X3

Not valid to current Harlequin Presents subscribers.

Want to try two free books from another line?
Call 1-800-873-8635 or visit www.morefreebooks.com.

---

* Terms and prices subject to change without notice. NY residents add applicable sales tax. Canadian residents will be charged applicable provincial taxes and GST. This offer is limited to one order per household. All orders subject to approval. Credit or debit balances in a customer's account(s) may be offset by any other outstanding balance owed by or to the customer. Please allow 4 to 6 weeks for delivery.

Your Privacy: Harlequin is committed to protecting your privacy. Our Privacy Policy is available online at www.eHarlequin.com or upon request from the Reader Service. From time to time we make our lists of customers available to reputable firms who may have a product or service of interest to you. If you would prefer we not share your name and address, please check here. ☐

HP07

Inside ROMANCE

Stay up-to-date on all your romance reading news!

Inside Romance is a FREE quarterly newsletter highlighting our upcoming series releases and promotions.

Visit

www.eHarlequin.com/InsideRomance

to sign up to receive our complimentary newsletter today!

IRN11O7

HARLEQUIN®

Mediterranean
N I G H T S™

*Sometimes you need someone to teach you the
things you already know....*

Coming in February 2008

CABIN FEVER

by

Mary Leo

Vacationing aboard *Alexandra's Dream* with her
two kids and her demanding mother-in-law,
widow Becky Montgomery is not about to start
exploring love again. But when she meets Dylan
Langstaff, the ship's diving instructor, she realizes
she might be ready to take the plunge....

Available wherever books are sold
starting the second week of February.

www.eHarlequin.com   HM38968

Harlequin Presents would like
to introduce brand-new author

Christina Hollis

and her fabulous debut novel—

ONE NIGHT IN HIS BED!

Sienna, penniless and widowed, has caught the eye
of the one man who can save her—Italian tycoon
Garett Lazlo. But Sienna must give herself to him
totally, for one night of unsurpassable passion....

Book #2706

*Look out for more titles by Christina, coming soon—
only from Harlequin Presents!*

www.eHarlequin.com

HP12706

HARLEQUIN *Presents*

THE ROYAL HOUSE OF NIROLI

Always passionate, always proud.

**The richest royal family in the world—
a family united by blood and passion,
torn apart by deceit and desire.**

By royal decree Harlequin Presents is delighted to bring you
The Royal House of Niroli. Step into the glamorous, enticing
world of the Nirolian Royal Family. As the king ails he must
find an heir.... Each month an exciting new installment
follows the epic search for the true Nirolian king. Eight heirs,
eight passionate romances, eight fantastic stories!

A ROYAL BRIDE AT THE SHEIKH'S COMMAND
by Penny Jordan
Book #2699

A desert prince makes his claim to the
Niroli crown.... But to Natalia Carini
Sheikh Kadir is an invader—he's already
taken Niroli, now he's demanding her
as his bride!

www.eHarlequin.com · HP12699